Praise for
FRANK SINATRA IN A BLENDER

"Matthew McBride is one of those rare writers who can have you reeling in shock one minute, and laughing out loud the next. *Frank Sinatra in a Blender* is a prime example. This book is a fun, twisted romp through McBride's uniquely warped imagination. I loved every minute of it."
—John Rector, national bestselling author of *Already Gone*, *The Cold Kiss,* and *The Grove*

"*Frank Sinatra in a Blender* is a darkly shining example of psycho noir that takes it to the wall and then straight on through. Stark, startling, extreme, haunting, and even poignant at times, the work of Matt McBride is going to be talked about for years to come."
—Tom Piccirilli, author of *The Last Kind Words*

"There's a great line toward the end of this book where Nick Valentine says, "A chainsaw cuts best when it's operated at full throttle." And that's what this book is: a chainsaw operated at full throttle. And damn if he's not right, it *does* work best. This is a violent hell-trip of a book full of drugs and drink and bad people you like as soon as you meet 'em. Make no mistake, McBride is the king of Chainsaw Noir, and there's no one else who can step to the throne."
—Chuck Wendig, author of *Blackbirds* and *Mockingbird*

"*Frank Sinatra in A Blender* is a perfect mix of hardboiled fiction and pulp noir—with a dash of Hunter S. Thompson. To say I loved this book is an understatement."
—Brad Wyman, Hollywood film producer of *Freeway* and *Monster*

FRANK SINATRA IN A BLENDER

Matthew McBride

A NEW PULP PRESS BOOK

First Printing, December 2012

Copyright © 2012 by Matthew McBride

This book is a work of fiction. Names, characters, places, and
incidents either are the products of the author's imagination or are
used fictitiously, and any resemblance to actual events or persons,
living or dead, is entirely coincidental.

ISBN-13: 978-0-9855786-0-2

ISBN-10: 0-9855786-0-2

Printed in the United States of America

Visit us on the web at www.newpulppress.com

To Charlie Sheen
for winning

FRANK SINATRA IN A BLENDER

INTRODUCTION

Ken Bruen

How important is a title? These days, vital. So many books vying for attention and, according to the experts(!), a book gets less than five seconds in a display to grab your interest. The cover, sure, plays a large part but it's the name, especially for a new author.

Take the ever-fascinating title—*By Grand Central Station, I Sat Down and Wept.* Then and now, an arresting rivet.

Matthew McBride was inspired when he wrote down his title.

I have to 'fess up. Books sent to me to read as an attachment are not going to be a priority. More like duty, so they are already handicapped. I'm a Luddite; I like clocks, mobile phones, people to be: Simple Accessible Portable.

And books: No e-book Kindle. What the hell ever is going to give the rush of a book in hand, the binding, the feel, the reassurance of an old friend?

Rod Wiethop, a cherished friend and connoisseur of music and mystery, asked if I would read a debut novel. For Rod, sure, *but hey, don't hold your breath, it wasn't going to be anytime soon.*

Until I saw the title. Intrigued, I figured I'd sneak a peek and perhaps, even subject it to the Page 69 Test.

Wallop.

I was hooked. And got that frisson of being in the presence of something special. There is not a reader on the planet who doesn't relish, anticipate, hope to discover a new author, to be there for the very first book.

It's rare to rarest found. Twice in my experience. Only Jim Crumley and Daniel Woodrell fulfilled that criterion for me. And here was Matthew McBride. Best of all, I knew nothing, *nada,* about the author, so I read him, if not cold, at least without reservation. And oh how sweet the growing joy of realizing this was indeed the real deal. Ticking all my personal data in your face: hilarious, fresh, innovative, and a style so crafted, it seemed easy.

To reveal the plot, the narrative, would be a true disservice. The magic of this book is to read it as I did, fresh and in the dark. Trust me, you will be fully rewarded. This is, to paraphrase a cliché, an offer you'll be delighted you accepted.

Ken Bruen
—Morocco, April, 2011

"Alcohol may be man's worst enemy,
but the Bible says love your enemy."

—Frank Sinatra

I pulled into Norman Russo's driveway as the sun was seduced by gravity and evening set in. Orange and pink stripes blazed then faded in the dead sky behind his neighbor's shed, in desperate need of paint.

I let the Crown Victoria run while I finished the rest of my drink and set the Styrofoam cup next to the short-barrel shotgun mounted on the floorboard. I dropped a 20-milligram Oxycontin in the middle of a dollar bill, folded the bill up tightly, and smashed the pill to a fine powder with the rounded edge of a Bic.

I rubbed the paper between my fingers to grind it up as best I could.

The car shook as the wind slammed it from the side. I looked around. There were two empty police cruisers parked in front of me and an officer lighting up a smoke on the front porch.

I dumped out the powder and rolled up a bill tight, then ducked down to snort a line half the length of the owner's manual for a 1997 Crown Victoria.

When the Oxy hit, my right eye began to water. I sniffed hard and took another drink of gin. I opened my door and the cold wind sawed deep into my bones. Chemical motivation cleansed my nerves as the world inside my head exploded and painted my mind with raw enthusiasm.

Norman Russo picked a good day to kill himself. The weather was shit and there was nothing worthwhile on TV. Not that I watched much of that. I had better things to do. Like drink.

I nodded toward the rookie at the door like I was someone important. It worked. He gave a nod of his own. I should have brought my cup.

The house was clean and had the look of a place with money. A nice home in an expensive neighborhood, meticulously maintained except for that peeling shed. An officer was taking pictures of the sliding door with a digital camera. I noticed there was no security system.

Another officer asked who I was. I told him I'd been summoned by the Chief, that they should've been expecting me.

"Valentine?"

I nodded.

"Right over there." He pointed toward a set of stairs with a hole knocked in the drywall above. Splinters from the two-by-four Norman Russo used to hang himself from decorated the staircase carpet.

It looked like the victim killed himself on the staircase. Not the first place I would've picked.

"Down here," a voice shouted from the basement. Another officer squeezed by me in the hall as if I were invisible. They resented the fact that Chief Caraway called me down to observe.

When I took the first step down, unexpected elation blistered inside me as the Oxy invaded my system. I stopped midway down the stairs to get a closer look at the suicide note pinned to the wall with a yellow thumbtack. The writing was sloppy at best and hard to read, like it was written in haste.

I heard a familiar voice behind me and turned to find Dan O'Shea, a veteran detective I knew from way back.

"What do you think, Nick?" Dan's wide shoulders and concrete-hard chest reflected his former career as a boxer.

I swallowed and cringed as the remains of the Oxy drained down my throat, then told him it was the funniest suicide note I'd ever read.

O'Shea stood in the doorway, perplexed. "Well, that's a helluva thing to say."

I looked down at the lifeless heap of body on the bottom step and shrugged. Told O'Shea maybe the deceased was just a bad speller. He shook his head and searched for a response that never came.

It was hard to believe a 300-pound man would hang himself from a rafter over the basement stairs with a rope that didn't look strong enough to string a piñata. When I got close to the body Russo's neck sure looked broken. But there was bruising around the upper spine that didn't come from a rope. I knew something about rope. It looked like somebody'd beat him across the back and neck with a bat. I knew about bats too. Knew what an aluminum Easton was capable of in the hands of a gifted slugger.

Starting with a handwritten suicide note that didn't make sense, my suspicions of the crime scene were strong and unwavering.

I walked outside through the basement door and stepped into the last rays from the retreating sun. The icy wind made me wish for a cup of hot coffee in my hand, but I had quit. Thoughts of coffee made me long for a cigarette but I had quit those too. In fact, the cigarettes were why I quit the coffee; I couldn't have one without the other. It's all or nothing for a guy like me. A guy who appreciates funny suicide notes.

Back on the road I began to think about the things I'd seen and all the parts that didn't make sense. It all started with the phone call I'd received from the Chief asking me to go down and take a look. He couldn't get away himself and wanted an experienced set of eyes he could trust to take things in.

After seeing the way those dipshits operated I could understand why.

I used to be a cop and I loved what I did but the job didn't love me back. But I still had connections on the force and the right people liked me. A private detective can make enough dough to scrape by as long as people keep raping, cheating, and killing each other. Lately I didn't seem to have any lack of work.

I got back to my office by late afternoon and put a cold Corona in my hand and my feet on the desk. The thermostat was stuck on high and a fan blew warm scorched air in my face with barely enough force to part my hair. My office was searing but I was reluctant to open any windows. In this part of town you never knew who might see an open window as an open invitation.

I dropped the empty bottle into my aluminum wastebasket and the unfinished suds spewed out and washed over one of Frank Sinatra's turds. It was a long way down to the street. Sometimes I let Frank shit on the floor.

Frank Sinatra was my Yorkshire terrier—half Yorkshire, the other half was something else. I'd only seen his mother once; she'd been the Yorkshire. The father was a stray who only came around when mama's scent was in the air. Frank was a bastard just like me.

"C'mere, Frank."

Frank was sleeping on his back with all fours in the air, content with the lifestyle of unscheduled napping only a dog can know.

"Frank," I said, then whistled. His ears popped up. He rolled over and was on his way toward the sound of my voice before he realized what was happening. He locked up his brakes, slid across the cheap tile floor, and bounced off the bottom of my chair. He took a few awkward sleepy steps to one side, then sneezed.

I patted my leg and Frank sprang onto my lap, managing to land right on my balls like he always did. "*Goddammit, Frank!*" Frank didn't care. He jumped around, snorted, and licked his lips.

I grabbed a Corona from the mini-fridge I kept close and popped the cap with the bottle opener mounted on my desk. I did it all with style.

Frank jumped down and ran a circle around my chair, tripping over one of the legs but managing to catch himself in an extraordinary display of coordination.

I watched as a fast gasp of beer escaped the mouth of the bottle and ran down the side, hugging the glass tight. I tipped the bottle slowly and let the beer spill into my mouth.

I thought about the dead man at the bottom of his staircase. The one who couldn't spell.

Nobody walked away from a life like that without a better reason than the one his note suggested. I just couldn't believe that Norman Russo was smart enough to manage a bank but dumb enough to hang himself above a staircase using weak lumber and cheap rope. Something didn't add up. Not to mention that suicide note telling his soon to be ex-wife she could have the horse.

Norm didn't have a horse.

His *house* was currently the center of attention in a messy divorce. But still.

Nobody kills himself over a house.

At least I didn't think so. I dropped the empty bottle into the trash where it clinked hard against another but didn't break. That's one thing I've gotta say about Corona—they know how to make a tough bottle. I know this because I've hit people with them.

Frank's little toenails went *click, click, click,* on the broken tile and he wrestled with the tongue of his favorite toy: a faded green Chuck Taylor Converse that was bigger than he was. He threw himself in reverse and started pulling the tattered shoe across the floor.

When I opened my bottom drawer, Frank stopped dead in his tracks. His fuzzy little ears shot straight up in the air and his mouth parted far enough that I could see a few teeth. Frank knew the sound of the drawer and had a clear understanding of what that sound meant for him. He froze. He wanted to be absolutely sure of what he suspected was about to happen before he put out the energy to run. He turned his head to the side to investigate.

Frank's tail was whipping from left to right and he gave out a few lively snorts. He was ready for breakfast.

I'd cut the top off a Bud Light can to scoop his food from the bag. I looked around but couldn't find his bowl. He liked to drag it off to his corner. Sometimes I'd just dump his food in his shoe.

I told Frank to bring me the shoe but it was too late. His legs were already moving and I had the beginnings of a nice beer buzz so I wasn't getting up.

All four legs were spinning and his nails were clicking. Then he started with his serious bark, the one that meant business. Frank was on a kibble mission, his belly rumbling.

He couldn't get there fast enough. I just dumped the food out on the floor in the same spot I usually did when he didn't bring his shoe.

Overwhelmed with excitement, he slid into the pile and the food scattered in all directions like a hand grenade full of dog food had just gone off. Then he grabbed a few choice pieces and made his way to his eating spot, the place on the other side of my desk where the tile met the dirty, worn-out carpet that hadn't seen a vacuum since the day I'd started paying rent.

I grabbed my third bottle from the mini and leaned the chair back as far as it would go. I thought about a cigarette but knew I was stronger than that. I pried off the cap, let it drop into the can, and drained half the beer by the time Frank returned for another bite. Maybe I could get away with this for the rest of the night. I glanced at the clock and realized the batteries were dead.

I just needed to shut my eyes for an instant to rebuild my strength but I woke when the bottle dropped on the floor and rolled under the desk. Frank wasted no time as head janitor and went to town on that spillage like the alcoholic he'd one day grow up to be. At some point after that I drifted into a dreamless slumber and left the dog to his custodial duties.

Telly woke up on the couch to the sound of his phone vibrating across the glass coffee table and didn't want to pick it up.

But he would, he had to. The man he worked for wasn't the type to leave a voicemail.

Telly glanced over at the television and saw a nice set of

tits that helped get his attention. Then two sets of tits. Girls started kissing and Telly sat up.

"Yeah?" he answered.

"It's about fucking time asshole. Been callin' ya all night."

It was Bruiser, of course.

"Hey, you awake tough guy?" His New York accent sounded practiced and counterfeit.

More nakedness flickered on the TV as Telly pulled himself up to the coffee table and searched for the remote. The girls were now fully nude and a blonde in pigtails was about to go down on the brunette in high heels.

"Hey, listen up you prick," Bruiser continued. "Today's a big day y'know."

Telly was distracted by the TV. Now a gunman stormed the room and shot both of the naked girls. Telly winced. *What the fuck was he watching?*

"Listen up, I ain't gonna tell ya again. I'm just gonna come up there and shoot'chya."

"Okay, okay," Telly said. "Come up? What the fuck, man? You outside?"

"Course I'm outside," Bruiser said. "Look out your fuckin' window." Bruiser was talking in his trademark jerk-off tone.

Telly shuffled across the living room and peered through the glass. He saw Bruiser leaning against the side of his Cadillac. Cell phone in one hand, cigarette in the other.

Telly waved and Bruiser said, "Get down here you pole smoker, we got shit to do."

"What time is it?"

"Time to go to work you lazy fuck. Now g'down here."

Telly closed his phone and walked back across the living room. The gunman on TV was now eating a sandwich.

It takes a pretty big set of balls to rob a credit union in a bread truck. An inconspicuous ride, but it's never going to outrun anybody. Telly sat behind the wheel with a scanner in one hand, a portable radio in the other, and the corner of a baggie filled with pinkish-white powder resting on his leg. He set the scanner on the dash and uncurled the twisty from the baggie, held it with his teeth. He tapped with his finger and knocked a little crank out onto a brown plastic clipboard. He tied the twisty around the baggie tightly before sliding the bag of dope into the corner pocket of his jeans.

Telly smashed soft rocks to flat powder, then separated the pile and divided it into two thick lines. He pulled the end of a straw from his shirt pocket and set the clipboard down on the console. He collected his thoughts and savored the moment just before he took the hit. He put his head down, found the position, and sucked a powerful mix of ephedrine, ether, and anhydrous ammonia up his nose. He snorted hard, sat upright in the seat and pinched his nostrils tight. He embraced the scorching burn that raced up his nasal passages at lightning speed and found its way down the back of his throat.

"That's good shit! Oh that's good shit. Good shit!" Telly mumbled after that. His mind traveled to random and euphoric destinations now that his thoughts were free to meander where they wanted. He started thinking about the deck he'd build on the back of a house he drove by every day and always wished he owned. If only he had the money to buy that house. And if he ever *did* buy that house, he knew exactly how he'd be attaching that back deck. Or maybe it already had a deck.

He was tempted to drop everything and drive there right now, just to look.

If he just had that house, then he could build that deck. People'd come over for a get-together—BBQ, beer, horseshoes, swimming pool—all in the backyard of a house he knew, somehow, some way, he would own one day.

God he loved meth. It was enlightening and flawless. It took just one line to make every thought feel right inside his head.

He really wanted to see that backyard. He needed to know if it already had a back deck. If so, he'd be forced to reevaluate his entire line of irrational thinking.

The sound of the scanner jarred him out of his head. Cops were on their way. Somebody must've hit the alarm.

"The call went out, the call went out!" He yelled into the walkie-talkie.

The only response he got back was static and crackle. Gunshots followed.

"Fuck!"

Telly banged the side of his fist on the console but he was careful not to spill any meth. Even in a state of panic, preserving the dope was still a priority.

Pop, pop, pop! Telly jumped unexpectedly as bullets punched holes in the side of the bread truck and afternoon sunlight flared the dust motes that swirled the air.

"Fuck this!" Telly hit the engine and threw the truck in gear.

He looked out the side window and saw Bruiser making a run for it. A security guard laid down serious gunfire. Telly let off the gas and threw the door open as Bruiser jumped in, but not before taking two smoking rounds in the back.

He collapsed in the seat and died before Telly reached the stoplight.

A fourth round pounded into the back of the bread truck.

Telly weaved around a car while shifting gears, his right hand alternating between the stick shift and the strap of the enormous duffel bag that Bruiser wore slung over his left shoulder. The door was still open and Bruiser was about to fall out of the truck.

Telly was running out of street and needed to make a hard left. The tachometer was racing; he needed to shift gears. Telly let off the gas with his foot, pulled the bag his direction, let go, then stomped the clutch, grabbed the shifter and found fourth gear.

A Neon cut in front of him, and Telly hit its cheap plastic quarter-panel with the steel front bumper of the bread truck to push it out of the way.

"Fuck!" Telly screamed. "Watch where the fuck you're goin'!"

He finally pulled the duffel bag from Bruiser's shoulder, held it as tight as he could, then cut the big, awkward steering wheel hard to the left.

When the truck swerved, Bruiser fell hard to the right and disappeared through the open door. His body landed on the grimy asphalt shoulder of Peacock Street like a load of sod.

Cars honked and Telly watched in the side-view mirror as a truck ran over Bruiser's body. He winced. Sorry about that Bruiser. But he wasn't sorry. Bruiser was an asshole. With him out of the way suddenly, Telly could change his luck for the first time in his life. He'd keep all the cash for himself and move to a different city. Buy a big house with a nice back deck.

He threw the plan together but needed time to think. Meth and adrenaline sped through his system like two grades of rocket fuel and the pissed-off guy in the Neon was still right behind him, honking his tiny horn.

Telly had another two blocks to go. Two more blocks

until the Buick and the freedom to ditch the bread truck. The Neon kept riding his ass and drawing too much attention.

Telly found the alley and made a fast right, then turned the truck at an angle to block the alley. By the time he had the duffel bag in his hand, the guy from the Neon was pounding on the door and screaming about kicking Telly's ass.

Okay, then. Telly pulled a gun from his waistband and pointed it out the window at the Neon guy's mullet. "Get in the back, you motherfucker."

"Huh? *Whoa*, sorry man. It was probably my fault anyway." The Neon guy raised his hands and tried to back up, suddenly willing to forget all about it.

"Fucking right it was your fault, you dumb bastard," Telly sputtered. "*You pulled out in front of me!*" Telly jumped out and waved the gun around, played tougher than he was. He told Neon guy to climb inside the truck and walk to the back. "You fucked up now, man. Ya seen me."

"No really, it's cool. Look, I don't really care about the dent. It's just a Neon."

Telly smiled, showed his gold fronts. "Get in the truck right now, fuck face. You'll be fine."

Finally, Neon guy took his mullet and bad tattoos into the truck.

"I got my kid in the car, man. *Please*." His voice echoed in the back of the truck, full of racks of stale bread and now a trembling witness.

Telly glanced at the Neon and saw a car seat and a tiny figure strapped in it. He turned back and looked at the mullet guy. "Yep. He's a handsome one. Looks just like his daddy."

Telly raised the gun and shot him twice in the chest. A third round missed and went through a rack of wheat bread and tore through the side of the truck. His ears rang from the shots.

Telly took the straw from his pocket and reached back into the truck for the clipboard. He dropped down to one knee. Most of the crank was still on the clipboard. He snorted what was left but resisted the urge to lick. *No DNA left behind.* Telly was smart. He watched the Discovery Channel.

He wiped off the clipboard and tossed it in the back with the dead body and the smashed bread.

Telly slipped the straw into one pocket, the gun into another. He pulled a water bottle from the glove compartment and squirted gas on the driver's seat and dashboard. He sprayed the rest of the gas on the dead Neon guy, then tossed in a match.

Poof! The fireball warmed his face.

As Telly ran toward Park Avenue he heard screaming from the Neon.

I woke up on the couch with a blanket wrapped around my waist. Frank was sleeping soundly in a little burrow he'd created down between my feet. I'd been living in my office for the last few weeks. Too many problems with the landlord at my other place. I had a few issues with the neighbors, too. Seems they didn't appreciate me coming and going at all hours of the night.

When the Chief told me somebody called the station about screams coming from the basement I decided it was time to move. I brought a few things with me but I kept most of my belongings in a storage shed as I navigated my way through this phase of personal adjustment and transition.

I took a piss, brushed my teeth, shaved my face, took a shower, took a shit, made a pot of strong coffee, and kicked a petrified dog turd across the room with my bare foot—and it wasn't even noon yet.

I walked down the steps to get my newspaper from the sidewalk. Assuming there was a paper. I didn't have a subscription but more often than not I could find a paper if I looked hard enough.

I brought Frank along and let him do his business outside in the weeds. It's amazing how much piss a bladder that size can hold. For a dog as small as Frank, he never seemed to run out. After making his rounds and taking pisses too great in number to accurately record, his very last leg-hike produced nothing at all.

"I think you're outta juice, Frank."

He yapped once, then gave a powerful little snort.

"C'mon ya mutt."

He raced up the stairs ahead of me and waited outside the door of my office slash apartment doing circles.

Frank followed me inside where I dropped into my chair and heard the sound of its familiar screech under my weight. For me, this was the best moment of the day. A fresh cup of coffee, a smoke, and a scrupulous review of what was going on in my city courtesy of the *St. Louis Post Dispatch.*

Then I remembered I had just quit two of those three things I enjoyed so much.

I took a hard look at my favorite cup, empty now, and imagined creamy ripples across the surface. Four days without so much as a sip. I couldn't believe I was considering a cup of coffee. At least I couldn't smoke. Hadn't bought a pack of those cocksuckers in two weeks.

I took a deep breath and opened my paper only to find it was from the 15th of November and this was the 21st. That was the downside to a free subscription—sometimes you got yesterday's news. By now, the stories were old enough that I could read them again with only the slightest hint of *deja vu*. I stood up too quickly and my head began to spin. I was weak. I needed coffee and tobacco. In a perfect world I'd have both without guilt.

I threw my paper in the wastebasket and walked my coffee cup to the makeshift kitchen. I put the cup in its place next to the counter, which was little more than boxes stacked together to form a crude table.

Then I looked over at the device responsible for all this business in the first place and regarded my coffeepot with suspicion. I thought about destroying it but one look at the innocent face of my Bunn-o-Matic told me I could never find the strength. It's hard to define the relationship between a man and his coffeepot but I can say with complete honesty that this machine was the best friend I'd ever had.

In the end, I just didn't have the strength. She was a part of me and I was a part of her. I set her gently in the corner with the appliances and quietly beseeched the Java gods not to smite me for any momentary lapse in judgment.

I made a few calls before I left the office. I had a few questions for the Chief but the station said he was talking to reporters downtown. I said goodbye to Frank, who was busy mounting a Nerf football over by the boxes I'd come to think of as a kitchen table.

I told him to have a good time and closed the door gently.

I heard about the robbery on the radio. A credit union on Peacock and Stanley. They went in heavy—strong-armed and brazen. Ten in the morning and they were laying down gunfire on the sidewalk. The radio said a United Van Lines truck dragged one of their bodies down the highway.

Just another Tuesday in the city by the river.

I switched lanes at the next exit. I could see the TV news helicopters hovering a few blocks from the Arch. Traffic would be backed up. I took a slow drink from the Corona clenched between my legs and watched the cars around me. Someone in this city just stole a lot of money and I wanted to find them. It was only a matter of time before the street would summon the truth.

I parked two blocks away and left the Vic with the Styrofoam cup in my hand. I drank warm Corona through an orange plastic straw. I took my time and watched all the faces in the crowd clumped on the sidewalk in front of the stores.

The body lay under a tarp surrounded by cones, sawhorses, and yellow police tape. The officers guarding the area seemed more concerned with providing good camera angles than protecting the integrity of the crime scene. Reporters were everywhere. Two helicopters whirled above us making wind. I saw a photographer I knew from back in the day snapping pictures of a torched bread truck. I crossed the street when I saw him and made my way to the truck.

Cameron Worthy was a photojournalist on the crime beat for the *Post Dispatch*. I knew him from my days on the force. He was a good enough guy. We had beers, exchanged information. Cam gave me the nod so I found a nice section of alley to hide in while I sucked beer through a straw and tried to keep the sun from my eyes. The November wind felt cold and sharp.

I took small steps until I was close enough to slip under the police tape and get a feel for what went down. A charred body under a sheet stunk up the bread truck, which sat next to a dented red Neon with an empty car seat sitting on the roof.

Still no sign of the Chief.

Cam walked up and said hello. "Nick Valentine? What brings you down here to the gutter?"

I would've held out my hand but it held my drink.

"How you doin', Cam?"

"Better than that son-of-a-bitch." He pointed to the van.

"Or *that* son-of-a-bitch." I pointed at the lump under the tarp.

Cam shook his head and pushed up his hipster glasses. They were too big and they slid down his nose. His long, thin hair blew in the breeze like an old T-shirt hanging on a summer clothesline.

I asked him what the hell happened here.

"Couple'uh guys hit that credit union and got away with major cash." He pointed south with his head as he slid a new smoke between his lips. "Guard capped one of them." He pointed toward the body in the road with his head again as he lit a Marlboro Light. "Other guy ditched the bread truck here. Guess they had another car waiting."

"What about this piece of shit?" I kicked the back tire of the Neon.

Cameron said he didn't know. He thought the driver was the crispy bastard in the bread truck. He said it looked like multiple gunshot wounds from up close, but don't quote him on that.

"So maybe the bread truck flees the scene and tags the Neon, then the Neon chases him down. The driver takes a few slugs in his chest in the name of road rage. Sound right?"

Cam said it did. Then he asked me if I wanted a smoke.

"No, thanks." I told him I quit.

"*Ouch.*" He took a long drag off his cigarette and scrolled through this morning's photos on his fancy camera.

I took a long drink of beer from my cup and the straw made a quick, violent noise against the plastic lid.

"Who robs a credit union in a bread truck?" he asked.

I said I didn't know. *Bakers?*

I scanned the area for surveillance cameras but there were none in plain sight.

"Nice place for a switch," I said, because it was. The alley was just a few blocks from the bank and was between a pair of major intersections. Easy access to multiple escape routes.

Cameron told me he had to get back to the newsroom. He dropped his smoke on the ground and crushed it with his dress shoe.

I told him I'd see him around and walked down the road toward the other body. I was finishing the last of my drink when I saw the Chief wave me down. I tossed my cup in a green metal trashcan.

The Chief's lips pressed against my ear. "How you doin', Nicky?" he asked. The Chief was the only one who called me that.

I told him I was getting by.

Chief Caraway and my old man went way back. They shared a twisted history of some kind but I never knew quite how deep the river flowed. If my old man were still alive I guess I could've asked him.

"This is a fucked-up deal, Nicky."

"Looks like it."

"They got away with a lotta money."

I shook my head, pretended like money didn't mean anything. But the Chief knew me better than that.

"Inside job?" I asked.

He was already nodding. "Had to be."

"Witnesses?"

"About a half dozen, but it went down pretty quick. Nobody saw much."

"What about that beat-up little shitter?" I pointed to the Neon.

The Chief told me two different people saw the bread truck ram the car from behind then the Neon chased the truck down.

"How big was the crew?"

"One man inside. One, maybe two more in the truck." Chief Caraway lit up a cigarette and smothered me in a second-hand cloud. I took a step back. You never realize how many people smoke until you stop.

My thoughts went back to the dead guy on the staircase. He was a banker. Could be a coincidence but probably wasn't.

The Chief's walkie-talkie started to squawk about the same time his phone rang.

"You have no idea what kinda shitstorm I'm dealin' with," he said.

I said nothing.

"Chief Caraway," he shouted into the phone, but covered the bottom with his hand and whispered to me. "What'd you find out yesterday? About that suicide?"

Before I could answer, he stuck his finger up, wanted me to wait a minute.

I wasn't sure how to play my cards without revealing too much. I still couldn't be sure what was what, I just knew something smelled funny and it wasn't the guy in the bread truck.

I said I had to run, told the Chief I'd see him later. The beer went through me quick and left me wanting more.

I found a dumpster to pee behind then I headed to the east side to a strip joint called Cowboy Roy's Fantasyland. I needed to see a guy about some business.

Telly drove an hour out of town until he found a dead-end road. He sat with the car in park and stared at the duffel bag that filled up the passenger seat. Telly watched nervously through the rear-view, sure that the cops were about to roll up on him—sirens screaming, guns drawn, bullets flying. His heart was racing and the excitement made him sweat. Or maybe it was the speed. He didn't know what to do first—look inside the bag of money or smoke a foily?

He pulled a baggie from the miniscule pocket above the right front pocket of his jeans, useless for anything except a small baggie of crank. He held the straw in his hand then had a better idea.

Telly pulled a box of Reynolds Wrap from under the seat and his mouth began to salivate. His palms sweated as he folded a crisp new piece of foil precisely. Like a veteran tweaker, his preparation ritual was an art form.

He emptied most of the baggie on the foil then cocked his head and poured a little more. Telly held the foil at just the right angle, and with the perfect mix of flame and wrist sent a clear pool of speed running down to the end. He inhaled the smoke through the hollow tube of an empty Bic pen then adjusted his hand as the boiling goo reached his thumb. Just as it hardened, he reversed the process and ran the trail back to the other end of the foil. His technique was beautiful.

Telly was a master when it came to smoking Bob White.

He thought about the indescribable taste of crank as he took the hit and held it, waited for a few seconds until his chest warmed, then exhaled a soft white cloud against the window and melted down into the seat. He stared up at the headliner of the car and waited for the magic to happen.

The gears inside his head were already grinding.

He noticed the material starting to sag above him; the cloth hanging low enough to touch his head. When he hit the foil again his brain shifted to a higher level of thought. A level he was incapable of reaching before the crank.

His world started to slow down when he ditched the bread truck but now it was all coming back fast. He was about to fall into that perfect groove of intellectual superiority that can only be achieved through excessive methamphetimine consumption. The more he thought about it, the more strongly compelled he felt to repair that headliner before it gave him any more trouble.

There was a toolbox in the trunk but Telly couldn't remember what tools he had back there. He couldn't remember the last time he looked. But maybe all he needed was a handful of well-placed tacks to do the job. Surely that would work, although he doubted whether he had any tacks. Or where they'd be if he did.

Telly put fire to the aluminum one more time then checked the rear-view again. He saw his eyes in the mirror. His dark, wet pupils turned the size of nickels. Then he thought about the money. *Yes, yes, the money.* He noticed the straw in his hand and stuffed it back into his pocket. Didn't want to lose that.

Telly needed to get his shit together and put things into perspective. He had to stash the money, get more crank, then decide how he was going to go about telling his version of the truth to the man he worked for. He would tell whatever version he thought sounded best, but that version was still up for grabs.

When he finally unzipped the bag and saw all the money that was his to spend, Telly couldn't move. He saw thousands of dollars. Could be millions but he couldn't possibly count it with any degree of accuracy.

Telly popped the trunk and pulled the duffel bag across the seat and let it drop onto the ground. Then he heaved it up to his shoulder in one spastic motion.

When he got to the back of the car, Telly threw the duffel in the trunk where it crashed into a plastic toolbox. The car shuddered. He thought for a moment about all those tools and the work he could do with them up front on that headliner.

Telly closed the trunk and rushed back to the driver's seat. He popped open his cell phone, saw it was low on minutes, and called the guy he got his shit from for the sixteenth time but of course he didn't answer. The man with the meth never answered the phone when you needed him to. Telly turned up the heater. He was cold but sweating. Telly would need to call English Sid before long, but he was a wreck. He just needed crank first—had to have it.

Telly started the car and turned around. He needed to see a guy he knew about some business.

I pulled into Cowboy Roy's Fantasyland and parked next to a Lincoln Town Car that belonged to Anthony Sparrow, though everybody called him Big Tony. Big Tony knew a lot of things about a lot of things. I was confident he'd know a thing or two about the credit union job.

I passed through the front door and Flames, the bouncer, gave me a nod. He told me I was good and I asked him if he'd seen Big Tony.

"He's in the back," Flames said. "He'll be right out."

I thanked him and we went our separate ways. We both had more important things to do than chat each other up. Besides, I needed a drink.

A brunette who smelled like cocoa walked by and gave

my package a casual squeeze, as if we were in a supermarket and my dick were an avocado. "Hey, Nick," she said. I thought her name was Lilac but hell if I could remember. I watched her hard, tight body move as she made her way to the end of the bar.

"Whaddaya need, Valentine?" Flames was standing behind the bar mixing drinks.

I did a double take. "What? You're tendin' bar too?"

Flames shrugged, said it was hard times and all.

I told him I wanted a Scotch. Neat. Two shots of Crown Royal and a bottle of Corona with lime. He didn't say a word, just set me up and walked off like a good bartender should.

A thick cloud of fake smoke swept across the stage. I did the first shot of Crown then chased it with the second shot, followed by a long drink of beer. I squeezed the lime into my mouth and took a shallow breath. *Fuck me.* The rush almost knocked me over.

I helped myself to a barstool and started working on that Scotch. I hadn't been to Cowboy Roy's in at least a month and it seemed like the scenery was always changing.

Another big drink and I could see brown liquor disappearing from my glass as the first hard rush of a wicked, nut-busting drunk came on strong. I looked around for Lilac. Started thinking about her firm, uncompromising body.

I turned and looked for Flames and told him, "Set me up one more time."

Flames looked at me funny and I watched his eyes grow with curiosity. "*Jesus*, that was fast."

I told Flames I was thirsty. "When it comes to drinking I don't fuck around."

Then Big Tony came out from the back room. He was walking by himself, sniffing. It was a safe bet his bushy mustache was covered with a nice white dusting of blow.

Big Tony saw me and veered over. We shook, his big paw swallowing my hand. He asked me what I was up to.

"What do you know about this thing downtown earlier today?"

Big Tony told me he didn't know shit. "Ain't heard much about it."

I grabbed my Scotch and beer and followed Big Tony to his table. A waitress in a camouflage bandanna and an American flag g-string paused in front of him and he whispered something rude in her ear. His face was up against her ear. He sniffed her like a fine Barolo.

Bandanna Girl said she'd be right back, but when she walked away I could tell she wanted to bathe in disinfectant the first chance she got to eradicate the thin layer of funk that clung to her just from being in the presence of such clientele.

Present company excluded.

Big Tony took a seat while I took a hard hit of Scotch, then set the glass and the Corona bottle down on the table. I sat across from him and asked what he knew about Norman Russo.

Big Tony shrugged. "Who the fuck is that?"

I told him I didn't know. Maybe just some fuck.

"What's he into you for, Valentine?"

"He ain't into me for nothin'," I said. "He's laid out right now with a *Y* carved in his chest."

"Dead?" Big Tony asked.

"Yep. Gettin' autopsied right now."

The waitress in cammo returned with a well-rehearsed smile and I realized at once that I had a strong appreciation for her breasts.

She gave Big Tony a bottle of Pabst, the cheapest beer they had. He paid her with a five and said keep the change.

She asked me what I wanted.

"A shot of Yukon Jack, a shot of Wild Turkey, and an ice-cold Corona," I told her, laying out the demands of a free-range drinker. "Don't forget the lime." Drinking had always been important to me and I did it with as much enthusiasm as possible.

Big Tony lit a cigar and took a drink from his PBR. He set a little box on the table, opened it up, set out a mirror, then dumped powder on the glass. He asked me if I wanted a line. I told him I'd better not, but I didn't like the way he looked at me when I said it.

To avoid drawing suspicion, I thought I should probably go ahead and indulge just this once. I could always debate the finer points of the issue later. I'd made a promise to myself about the coffee and the cigarettes, but I never said anything about turning down cocaine.

He did his rail first, the longest one, of course, which ran a good six inches. Then he pushed the mirror my way. It said Cowboy Roy's Fantasyland across the top but the line he left for me was only long enough to reach from the *R* to the *Y* in *Roy*. I snorted it and embraced the familiar numbness like a handshake from an old friend. It was the electric cherry on top of my drunk buzz. But still, the cheap bastard could've put out just a little more.

A few minutes passed and we talked about all kinds of things before Bandanna Girl made it back with our drinks. She brought him another PBR and he thanked her with a friendly slap to her perfect ass, a humiliating gesture she hated but had to endure if she wanted to get paid.

Big Tony worked his game on the dancer with insufficient skill. While an obvious exercise in futility, it turned out to be the best part of my day. He never had a chance with any of his girls, a fact everyone seemed aware of except him.

I downed the shot of Yukon Jack like a champ. Then

followed it with the Wild Turkey. *101 proof.* It tasted like kerosene going down and started a bonfire in my guts.

A stripper walked on the stage and took her panties off and every pair of eyes in the club was raping her at once. When the earsplitting bass paused, I heard the familiar sound of a razorblade dragging small piles of blow across glass. The cocaine chased the Oxy through my system, followed by plenty of liquor. I realized suddenly that I had to get out of Roy's before I passed out cold or jumped on stage and dragged the stripper to the back like a caveman.

That last shot of Wild Turkey must've really turned me sideways. Something didn't feel right. I focused on the door and reminded myself to slow the fuck down.

When I stood up, I knocked over my chair and the blood rushed to my head like it always did when I moved fast. I leaned down, put my hands on the table and righted myself. I told Big Tony I was out. He told me to call him tomorrow, said maybe he'd know something.

I threw a twenty, a ten, and a wad of one-dollar bills on the table and headed for the door. Big Tony yelled something at me but I couldn't hear anything but the rap music that was thundering from the overhead speakers.

I passed Flames as I shouldered my way through the crowd and he gave me a casual nod.

Then I bounced into some asshole who wasn't looking where he was going either. I hurried out the door. Neither one of us said sorry.

Winter ice was coming and the air was dry and thin. Leaves no longer fell and the ones that lined the street were brown and dead. Parked by a dry cleaners, Sid Godwin watched the traffic and scanned mobile porn on his iPhone. He knew the boys weren't coming. Bruiser was dead, but what about Telly? He was two hours late. Telly might be on the run or he might be dead too.

Sid scrolled through the menu of options on a site that offered everything from straight sex to midgets jacking off donkeys, which was pretty much the last thing he ever wanted to see. Still, maybe it was worth looking into.

Just as the page opened, the words *No Nuts is calling* flashed across the screen and broke the connection. Sid answered "Goddammit, Johnny," in his thick British accent.

Johnny No Nuts asked what he did wrong this time.

"Nothin'," Sid said. He asked him if he'd heard any news.

Johnny said he hadn't. He was hungry, said he was going for some food.

Sid sat up in his seat. He couldn't believe what he was hearing.

"Now listen here mate, you're doing no such fucking thing. You're gonna sit there and wait like a good lad. Keep your eyes open. Watch for Telly in the Buick."

No Nuts said he would, then hung up.

Johnny No Nuts was as useless as tits on a fish. But Mr. Parker loved him, even tagged him with his nickname in the first place.

Johnny No Nuts was a gutless turd, but at the end of the day he was funny. Damn funny. And that reason alone kept him alive this long. He was a comedian.

Sid got tired of sitting in the lot too but they couldn't leave until they got the word from Mr. Parker. He called the shots. There was a lot riding on this deal and Sid wasn't going to be the one to fuck it up.

Sid's phone rang again. It was Telly.

"Yeah?" Sid answered.

Telly was all worked up and out of breath. "Sid? Hey man, where you at?" He was talking fast, rambling. "Everything got all fucked up, Sid. Bruiser got wasted, he's dead." Then he told Sid he didn't have the money.

Sid squeezed his phone almost hard enough to break it. He knew Telly was lying. They never should've used a tweaker.

"What do you mean you haven't got the money, Telly?"

Telly paused. "I mean I ain't got it, Sid. *I never had it!* Bruiser barely made it to the car. He's layin' back there in the street, man."

"Car? You used a bloody bread truck you stupid bastard. It's all over the news."

"Car, bread truck, *what-the-fuck ever*, man."

Sid was quiet. Said, "Lemme think."

Telly went on. "Bruiser's dead, man. I gotta get the fuck outta here. I'm hot, Sid. I gotta get outta the city, man."

Sid told him no. "You're not goin' anywhere till we talk to Mr. Parker. He ain't gonna like this."

"Fuck him!" Telly said. "I'm scared, Sid. I just saw Bruiser get smoked. I still got his blood all over me."

"Hey, not over the phone!" Sid ordered. "Meet me at Montgomery's in an hour."

Sid hung up and put in a call to Mr. Parker. Then he called Johnny No Nuts and told him to get the church ready.

"Grab a few bags of ice and a couple of buckets. Grab somethin' from the Burger House too, if you want. We're gonna be busy for a while." Sid left the dry cleaners and drove to Montgomery's.

Telly was walking into Cowboy Roy's Fantasyland as he hung up the phone with Sid. As he walked through the door, he bounced off some asshole in a hurry to leave. He scanned the room with desperate eyes until he found the man he was looking for.

He walked up to the table and slid into an empty chair across from a huge Italian guy with a pile of dark hair on top, brown wasted eyes, and a bottle of Pabst Blue Ribbon in the grip of his chubby hand.

"Hey, how ya doin' Tony?"

Big Tony regarded him with suspicion and lit a cigar. He asked Telly what he wanted.

Telly looked around, scratched at his arms. "Hey, man, I'm lookin' for some shit, if you know what I mean." He paused. "Some crank."

Big Tony gave him a smart look. Asked him what the fuck he was talking about.

"C'mon man. *I know* you can find that shit, Tony. I'm desperate here, man. I need it bad."

"What do I look like, shitbird? I don't know nothin' about whatever it is you think I know."

"*Oh, that's bullshit man!*" Telly pounded the table with his fist. "C'mon man, *I got money!* Just hook me up, bro." He produced three crinkled one hundred dollar bills from his pocket and tossed them in front of Big Tony. "See man, I got money."

Big Tony grabbed the money and jammed it in his shirt pocket.

"Whutchya want, Telly?"

Telly's eyes were untamed, jumpy.

"What do I want? *I want dope godammit!* C'mon, man."

"Okay," Big Tony said. "Calm the fuck down. I'll see what I can do."

"Yeah, please. Just make a call or somethin'," Telly begged.

Big Tony looked around, lowered his head. "How much you wantin'?"

"As much as you can get, Tony. An ounce. A pound, whatever. I got the money."

Big Tony couldn't believe this bullshit. Telly was a tweaker. He didn't have squat. He couldn't believe he had three hundred dollars on him. But it sounded like he had more.

"An ounce?" Big Tony asked sarcastically. "*A pound*, Telly? A motherfucking pound of crank? Are you high?"

Telly shook his head. "Yeah, I know it's a lot, Tony. I do. It's a lot. But I got the money, man. I got the money. I just need this if you can help me, then I'm gettin' the fuck outta here."

Big Tony nodded his head like he understood. But the only thing he understood was that Telly must be involved in something heavy. Tony had to find a way to separate him from whatever money he had and do it quick.

"What're you into Telly?" He thought about the credit union job, but it seemed like a stretch.

Telly's eyes scavenged into the dark corners.

"C'mon Telly, sounds like you're in over your head, man. Maybe I can help."

Telly blinked his eyes, snorted air. Said all he needed was crank and he'd pay top dollar for it if Big Tony pulled through.

"I'll see what I can do." Big Tony said he'd make a few calls. Told him an ounce was a lotta weight. He'd need to see more cash before he got involved.

Telly said, "No problem." He pulled a wad of bills from his pocket and did a piss-poor job of trying to hide them as he counted under the table. He slapped five hundred down, pushed it over to Big Tony. "I'll meet you in an hour. Crestwood Bowl, you know it?"

Big Tony said he did. He told Telly he'd see what he could do. Eight hundred was a nice start, but he couldn't get that much in an hour. There was just no way.

Big Tony tested him. "What if I really could find a pound? You ain't got that kinda cash, I know."

Telly laughed. "Trust me, man, I got plenty," he said. "You find me some shit right fucking quick if you're able and I'll pay ya more than I owe'n then some."

Telly jumped up from his seat without warning. Told Big Tony to get what he could, then body checked a waitress on his way out as she brought Big Tony his latest PBR.

Big Tony picked up his phone and started making calls.

When I opened my eyes I was sitting at a traffic light that had just turned green, with my foot on the brake, the radio blasting, and the blower from the heater on high. The window was down and my left arm was hanging out, dangling against the door.

Somebody somewhere was yelling. "Wake up, asshole!" Then he leaned on the horn.

I looked around and tried to get my bearings. I realized the light was now on yellow and about to hit red so I floored it. The tires barked hard, hooking up with the pavement and carrying the big car out into the intersection where I was almost hit broadside by some hipster in a Scion with a bicycle mounted to the roof.

He locked his brakes up, narrowly avoiding my Crown Vic. He waved his arms around and started honking.

I grabbed the brass knuckles that hung from the shifter and stuck my fist out the window. I wasn't sure how long I'd sat at that light, but I needed to piss, and I knew the mini-fridge was running dangerously low on alcohol. The Vic could use some gas while I was at it.

I pulled into the first station I saw and took a piss behind the car wash. I finished the rest of the Scotch I must have taken with me from the bar, then threw the empty glass up against a vacuum cleaner that ripped me off the one and only time I tried to clean the Vic.

With all the foresight a drunk in my position could manufacture, I decided to forgo gas. However, I did go inside and fulfill my commitment for more drink.

I walked out with a fifth of Southern Comfort, a bottle of rum, a frozen pizza, and two six packs of Corona. I climbed behind the wheel, set my bag into the seat, and pulled a stick of beef jerky from my pocket that I couldn't remember if I paid for. I thought about an ice-cold beer. I put the window up and out of nowhere started thinking about the credit union job.

Suddenly it all made sense and I was able to see it unfold in my mind with the absolute clarity that only an afternoon drunk at a strip joint can provide. Chief Caraway'd said all he knew about Norman Russo was that he managed a bank, but what if it was the credit union? Whatever assholes hit that credit union must have gone to Russo's house the night before. They pumped him for information and they killed him. Then they staged that suicide with a lack of professionalism unlike anything I'd ever seen.

I pulled the Vic onto the road and drove a few miles back to the office while I ran the scenario through my head. They used a crew of two or three guys. I was leaning toward a two-man crew. There'd only been one guy inside the credit union. There was no reason to have two getaway drivers unless they used a crash car, a driver in a second vehicle who could block the road just in case a cruiser arrived. But if that'd been the case, the crash car would've taken out the Neon.

Still, it was a pretty sophisticated job for just a few guys to pull off by themselves. And anybody smart enough to set this up *and* pull it off, would have to be smart enough to spell correctly.

When I climbed to the top step of my office I found a late notice taped to my door, across where it said Private Detective. I wadded up the note, slipped the key into the lock, then kicked the bottom of the door open with my foot.

Frank was there waiting. Snorting, sneezing, and turning circles.

"Hey, Frank." I stepped through the doorway carrying two bags. Frank was going crazy, jumping all around. He yelped when I stepped on his foot.

"Sorry." I went on to explain how this could easily have been avoided and was clearly his fault. I set both bags on the cardboard box I used for a table and carried both sixers over to the mini and loaded that bastard up. Frank started barking, giving me hell. I asked him if he had to shit.

"*Aaarp.*"

I grabbed the cordless from my office and took Frank outside so he could make his logs. There was a little area between the alleys with some grass. While Frank was busy, I put a call to the Chief but he wasn't in the office. I wasn't surprised, but I felt like I was working this whole damn case by myself. Maybe Big Tony'd come through. You never knew with him, but he was a guy I knew I could trust. He'd done hard time in the can and I respected that. Between Tony and his partner Doyle, they had their ears close to the street. They were plugged in.

Frank was sniffing everything and trying to saturate as many foreign objects as possible with his Yorkshire piss. He pissed on an old newspaper that was covered with other dogs' piss. He pissed on the handle of a shovel. He pissed on a brick. He pissed on top of another dog's old turd or perhaps it was his own. He even pissed on the seat of a little kid's Big Wheel. I would've told him to stop but I knew he wouldn't listen. Frank was just expressing himself and that was an idea I could get behind.

"Let's go." I whistled. Frank brushed past me in hurry to climb the stairs. If there was one true pleasure in Frank's life it was stair climbing. His favorites were the stairs to my office/apartment. And Frank's goal was to conquer them with as much speed and enthusiasm as his legs were capable of producing. He was a master of ascension, but coming back down had always been a problem. His body was too short and he would fall ass over teakettle. I coaxed him every chance I got, but Frank did things his own way. Generally I just carried him.

The drunk I'd put on earlier was all but a distant memory. With each step I took, I tried to wrap my head around this case.

Frank waited by the door. Tail wagging. Snorting. If he could've talked he would've told me to hurry up so I could throw a beer can full of kibble on the floor next to my desk.

"I'm comin'," I told him. He barked twice, snorted once, peeled out. Frank was ready and willing to take on the whole world if he didn't get food.

We entered my muddled office and I stared at its dismal state. I never had time to clean. As I succumbed to the comfort of my chair behind the desk, I knew I wouldn't have time today either.

Frank barked, told me he was waiting.

I said, "Yeah, I hear you already." I flipped on the little radio at the edge of my desk and we listened to some jazz.

I crossed the room and poured a beer can full of food in his Converse. Frank jumped, ran two complete circles around both me and the shoe, then bit the end of my pants leg and gave it a dominant tug.

"Calm down you little shit."

I kicked at him, nudged him away with my foot, something he didn't like, and he bit my shoe about as hard as he could. Snorted then peeled out. Frank took one good spring and landed on the Converse. He fought me for it, driving his snout deep into the cavernous depths of the shoe, giving it the business. He snatched a piece of kibble then ran to his place in front of my desk and dropped it. He looked up at me, growled, daring me to take it. Then he turned when I came near him and ate the kibble with his back toward me.

"You're a cantankerous little son-of-bitch." I dropped to one knee and stroked his back, but he turned with swift reflexes, barked twice, and told me not to fuck with him while he was eating.

I saw a bottle of Bailey's Irish Cream while I was down there, half full, sprawled on a bed of cigarette butts and ashes that'd been ground into carpet.

"Well, looky here," I said to Frank, but he was too busy eating.

I stood tall, held the bottle to the light and gave it a shake. I unscrewed the lid and knocked back a series of vigorous chugs.

Montgomery's was a steakhouse in South County where the cheapest steak cost thirty dollars. As bad as Sid craved a porterhouse, he didn't have the time to go inside. Mr. Parker was livid and he cursed the tweaker. He wanted to kill Telly, regardless of the outcome. That'd been Parker's plan all along. Use him as the driver and then shoot him; leave his body in the back of the truck.

Now there was a different asshole in the back of the truck. They were roaming down a thoroughfare of unknown possibilities, and too many roads led back to Mr. Parker.

Joe Parker was a businessman, thief, and gambler. If anything went down in St. Louis, he knew about it. Probably had a hand in it. The credit union job should have been a cakewalk. Instead, it was a clusterfuck. The wrong man was dead not to mention the unfortunate civilian casualty. Mr. Parker needed to cut the loose ends, starting with Telly. But first they had to ask him a few questions and see if he had the money.

It was Sid's job to ask him and he was going to ask him hard.

No Nuts pulled up beside Sid and they talked about what they'd heard on the street. There was no mention of the amount stolen, but the whole city was on alert. The cops were looking for a killer in the stolen bread truck. At least that's what the news said.

Telly was an hour late for the meeting when he finally pulled up in the Buick. No Nuts and Sid were surprised to see him at all. Telly parked, got out of the car and walked uneasily toward them.

No Nuts started in on him. "Where the fuck you been, cocksucker?"

Johnny was short. He wore a short suit and he always talked fast. He'd never had anyone to boss around and took full advantage of the situation now.

No Nuts slapped Telly on the top of his head to get his attention. "Where's the fuckin' money, ya prick?"

"Settle down, Johnny," Sid said calmly.

No Nuts looked around. He had the tweaker scared, had him right where he wanted him.

"Fuck this clown, Sid. I been waitin' out here in these cold weather conditions all fucking day for this guy."

"Hey, this is bullshit!" Telly argued. "I fucking got shot at man! *Shot at!* And I watched my buddy die right in front of me."

"Bruiser? It ain't like he was your pal. Ain't like you guys pitched horseshoes together or went bowlin'."

Telly shook his head and said that wasn't true at all.

"You're glad he's dead, you cocksucker! Now, where's that goddamn money?" No Nuts hit Telly with a solid uppercut under the ribs and Telly went to the ground.

"Okay, Johnny, calm down, boy." Sid stuck his arm out the window and tapped on the side of the door by Telly's head. "C'mon, Telly, jump in."

Telly looked up. Sid motioned with his hand. "Get in, Telly. We gotta take a little ride. Talk about this in the car."

Telly didn't want to.

"C'mon, get in." It was freezing. Sid put the window up and looked at Telly through the glass.

Telly knew he didn't have a choice. His best chance of not getting shot in the head was just to play along. They couldn't kill him, at least not until they knew if he had the money. By then he'd think of something.

No Nuts opened the back door and grabbed Telly by the arm. He pulled him off balance and patted him down. Checked him for weapons then shoved him headfirst into the back seat.

Sid laughed. Johnny was a big shot. Just the slightest hint of power went straight to his head.

He dropped into the passenger side and Sid turned the

radio up. 80s music on satellite radio and No Nuts couldn't stand it.

The breeze pushed the smell of Montgomery's sizzling meat through the car and No Nuts said, "I gotta eat somethin' Sid."

Sid turned the radio down with the steering wheel control. "I thought you ate, Johnny? I told you to hit the Burger House."

Johnny said he hadn't eaten. "The fucking line went around the block, Sid. 'Sides, I don't wanna burger. I'm tired of burgers. We eat burgers every day."

"I like burgers, Johnny."

"I like 'em too, Sid. But not every fucking day."

Sid shrugged. He asked No Nuts what he wanted.

"There's a great Mexican buffet down the road. I could use a chalupa."

Mexican sounded good to Sid but they had this piece of business first. The kind of business handled best on an empty stomach.

"I'm dyin' over here."

"Later, Johnny," Sid reminded him.

"I could eat too," Telly piped up from the back.

No Nuts turned around and stuck his finger in Telly's face. "You shut the fuck up asshole! Nobody asked you."

Sid cranked up the radio and sang "*We Built This City*", while he drummed his fingers on the steering wheel. No Nuts thought it sounded pretty gay with that accent.

I picked up the phone on the first ring, just because I was close. I expected Chief Caraway to greet me on the other end, but it was Big Tony. He said we should meet.

"Hey, you know that tweaker who runs with Bruno and those guys? Telly?"

I watched Frank drag his shoe across the room by the tongue. I couldn't picture anyone named Telly. *Or* Bruno for that matter. I told Big Tony I didn't know him.

"Yeah you do, Valentine. He works for Joe Parker. Big guy. Italian. 'Cept I dunno he's actually Italian."

I had no idea who he meant.

"Y'know, greasy lookin' hair. He's got this New York accent, but it sounds like shit. I hear he's from Kansas. He thinks nobody knows."

Suddenly I could see his face. It was the bad accent I remembered, like he'd spent years practicing it in front of the mirror.

"It's Bruiser," I said. "They call him Bruiser."

"That's it."

"What about him?" I wanted to know.

"Not him, that tweaker he runs with."

"Tweaker?"

"Yeah, Telly," he said. "You practically ran the guy over when you left Cowboy Roy's."

I thought about it, but it was really no use. As hard as I tried, I couldn't recall leaving Cowboy Roy's.

"You know who I'm talkin' about?"

"Yeah, sure," I lied. "What about him?"

Big Tony told me what happened after I left. The tweaker was in a tight spot. He was looking for crank; he wanted Big Tony to hook him up.

Big Tony said Telly was into something heavy, it could've been the credit union by the sounds of it.

"What'd you say?"

"I told him I'd see what I could do. Supposed to meet him here in a minute."

I slid my feet into my shoes and looked around for the keys to the Vic. I stuck a bottle of Corona in each pocket of my suit jacket and grabbed a yellow plastic cup from my cardboard table. I filled it with the four remaining cubes from my useless little ice tray. Then I grabbed a half-empty bottle of flat Mountain Dew from the mini and the bottle of Southern Comfort from my desk.

I made a drink, then said good-bye to Frank, who was crashed out in the corner with his chin on his Converse. I hurried to the Vic.

I met Big Tony at Crestwood Bowl. Doyle was sitting in the passenger seat of the Town Car. They looked to be in the middle of a deep conversation when I climbed into the back.

"Okay, boys, what's good?"

Doyle turned sideways in the seat. He had the look of a salesman to him, which he was. His rusty hair was turning gray at the edges and his smile spread wide over pudgy jowls. His brown suit looked stiff enough to stand on its own without a hanger, like the victim of a dry cleaning experiment gone wrong. He had the abrupt look of a guy you'd never want for a neighbor.

Doyle was a con man, a jewel thief, and a burglar. And he was good at what he did, connected with all the right people. The one guy you could count on to always be setting up scores.

I asked Doyle how he'd been and took a drink from my yellow plastic cup.

"Jesus, Valentine," he said. "You smell like a goddamn brewery."

I swallowed a mouthful of poison and told him I was out of cologne.

Then I told him what *I* thought. It looked to me like he should lay off the chilidogs. "Maybe you should ride a bike. Climb a few stairs." I thought about Frank when I said it.

Big Tony tried to turn sideways in his seat but he was bigger than Doyle. He grunted, hung his tongue from the side of his mouth like he was concentrating, but failed to actually rotate as far as I could tell. Defeated, he turned back toward the windshield and watched me through the rear-view mirror as he talked. He said they had some news.

"Sounds like Joe Parker's crew," Doyle said.

"Word is that dead guy in the middle of Peacock was that greasy fuck, Bruno," Big Tony added.

"Bruiser?" I asked.

"Yeah, him."

"That fuck with the goofy accent?"

"That fuck with the goofy accent."

I thought about this news and what it meant. A tweaker with that much cash wasn't long for this world. Somebody'd see to that.

"How much cash did that asshole Telly get?"

Big Tony threw up his hands. He didn't know. Doyle shook his head too.

I took another drink of Southern Comfort and Mountain Dew and thought about my next move. The picture was beginning to form in my head. Everything was coming together. Bruiser and Telly paid a visit to Norman Russo and they beat him to death with a baseball bat. Then they did a piss poor job of making it look like he'd killed himself. Telly probably wrote the suicide note.

"Well?" Big Tony asked.

I needed time to think. It was all happening fast and any

money recovered from the heist would be split three ways instead of one—something I didn't like, but accepted. I took the last mouthful of booze and the last two ice cubes shifted, sloshing drink on my face. I wiped my lip clean with my sleeve.

Doyle looked at me and I could tell they were going after the money with or without my help. My options were limited—work together or by myself. Three sets of eyes on the street were better than one. I shook the cubes together in my glass.

"Okay," I said. "I assume you have a plan?"

Doyle and Big Tony'd been putting their heads together. The plan they came up with was simple.

They'd show up at the meeting spot without the drugs and they'd rob him.

"*That's the plan?*" I asked.

Big Tony shrugged. "Works for me."

"Works for me too," Doyle agreed.

I pulled a Corona from the pocket of my sport coat and told Big Tony to turn up the heat.

The basement of the old church was bitter cold. A thick veneer of ice crusted the stained glass windows as each breath they took filled the room with heat for a moment. Telly's naked body was strapped to the metal chair. His feet were submerged in metal buckets of ice water that were nearly frozen solid around each foot.

"Lean him back," Sid ordered.

Telly was sickly pale white and shaking so badly his teeth crashed together when he tried for words.

Sid kicked the buckets out of the way when No Nuts tilted

him back and water washed over the floor. Mr. Parker had picked the building up at auction for a song. Now they just used it for storage or a place to cut up bodies.

"Hey dickhole!" No Nuts barked. He slapped Telly in the face to wake him up.

"Hear me in there?" No Nuts screamed. "You *will* talk to us."

Telly whimpered pathetically and cowered down as low as he could.

"Where's the money?" Sid demanded. "Don't fucking lie to me, cocksucker."

No Nuts opened his toolbox.

"C'mon Telly. Forget where you hid it already?"

Telly's expression turned blank. He searched for words to save him but his mouth was paralyzed by cold and fear.

"Remember?" Sid asked him.

No Nuts shrugged. "I don't think he remembers."

"Well, he'll remember being tortured," Sid said.

Telly thrashed about.

"Go head, yell if you want too. Ain't nobody gonna hear ya."

When No Nuts set the toolbox next to his feet, Telly really began to fidget.

"You look uncomfortable," No Nuts said indifferently as he removed a hammer. But it wasn't just any hammer. It was an eight-pound stainless steel industrial hammer. The kind you'd use for driving stakes into the ground to pitch a circus tent. It was brand new; No Nuts pulled the price tag off the handle with his teeth.

Sid had to admit it was an awe-inspiring tool. "Where'd ya get that bastard, Johnny?"

Johnny No Nuts smiled like a son who just tied his shoe right for the first time. His round face beamed with self-importance. The wrinkles around his eyes expanded when he spoke.

"Lowe's," he said with pride. "Got it from the Bargain Bin for $19.99."

"Son of a bitch that's cheap." Sid nodded quickly and raised an eyebrow in genuine approval for such a first-rate deal. He knew where he'd be getting his next hammer.

Telly shook uncontrollably now. His feet were frozen chunks of ice. He was slouching and trying not to cry. Sid grabbed him under his arms to raise him up. He tugged hard and some of Telly's ass skin ripped off and stuck to the frigid metal chair. The sound the skin made when it tore loose was clean and quick, like paper tearing.

Telly didn't like that, started screaming.

"Sorry," Sid told him, and he meant it.

Then No Nuts shattered Telly's right foot with the hammer and crushed his frozen toes.

The twenty-dollar hammer connected with tremendous force and Sid felt shock waves reverberate from the concrete up into his boots. Telly went crazy. His lurching caused more of his ass skin to bond with the chair and rip free. He expelled high-pitched, soaring notes that gave voice to his unbearable pain.

Then No Nuts raised the hammer.

Sid could see Telly's deformed pinkie toe stuck to the end of the hammer. They both laughed, and Sid told No Nuts to feed it to him.

No Nuts arched his eyebrows sharply and said it was a hell of an idea.

The look on Telly's face was one of genuine terror.

On impulse, Johnny pitched the toe into Telly's mouth as he howled and it went right in, triggering new laughter.

"Lucky shot," Sid told him.

Johnny said he knew it.

Telly spit the toe out with a force greater than a guy in his situation should've been capable of and it hit No Nuts in the chin. Another round of laughter followed. They were having fun. For a moment they forget how cold it was down in the basement, forgot about being hungry. Torture was a lot like quail hunting or bass fishing. While most would hesitate to call it a sport, there was just something about torturing a man that brought out the competitive nature in the two of them.

Sid took a step back from the situation, pulled a bottle of DeKuyper Blackberry Brandy from the pocket of his coat and let the thick syrup run down his gullet. He embraced the slight heat it gave then offered a shot to No Nuts.

Telly started cussing and yelling. He was pissed off about his toe but what he wanted more than another toe was another foily. His goal: live long enough to do more crank. He screamed at Sid and No Nuts. Told No Nuts to go fuck his mother.

Sid chuckled and Telly told *him* to go fuck his father.

Sid didn't like that; he was tired of Telly's mouth. He wanted to enjoy the precise second the brandy buzz found him and it was hard to fully appreciate the moment with Telly going on like he was. Sid grabbed the back of Telly's chair and pulled it across the floor until it set perfectly over the drain. He removed the handgun from its holster.

Telly's eyes flared abruptly. He did what everybody did in his situation. He started to beg. Wanted to make a deal. He said he had the money after all.

"Oh, *now* you have the money. If you had the money we wouldn't be here, ya wanker."

Sid pointed the gun at Telly, pushed the steel barrel against his cold flesh. Telly started farting. Profound, commanding flatulence that ricocheted off the metal chair in thunderous rounds. He said he was gonna shit himself.

"Okay," Telly screamed. "Okay, okay. I got it!" Spit jumped from his mouth. "Okay, I swear, I got it. I'm sorry, Sid. Don't fucking shoot me, I'll give it to you. We can split it three ways."

Sid shook his head from side to side. He told Telly no with his eyes.

Telly started crying. "*Look at my toes, you cocksuckers!*"

Sid took a step back and blasted a hot round into Telly's forehead. His body rocked back and forth, the chair balanced on two legs momentarily then fell on its side. Sid tried to keep the blood off his suit, but despite his slapdash precautions he still took considerable blood splatter.

Sid looked down at his suit jacket as he put the gun away. "Bloody hell."

Johnny laughed and said he wanted a taco, which was fine by Sid. It was getting late; he could eat. They'd just let Telly bleed out. They could always cut the body up after lunch.

W̶e waited at Crestwood Bowl until just after dark. There was no sign of Telly or the money. We listened to the scanner and the radio. As far as we knew he was still on the run.

With partial interest, I followed the Lincoln Town Car back to Cowboy Roy's. We needed to talk things over. Had to stay on this if we wanted to get paid.

I'd used a pay phone outside the bowling alley to call Chief Caraway. I asked him what he knew.

He said, "Them boys was either damn lucky or damn good." He asked me again what I knew about Norm Russo but I kept what I'd learned to myself. I still had a few angles of my own to work. I left out my involvement with Big Tony and Doyle.

The Chief told me, "Try a little harder. Do what you gotta do." He said it was important. Maybe if I broke this case he could pull a few strings. Said he'd like to see me back on the force.

When he asked about my drinking I told him it was under control, I was sober as a judge. And for a couple of hours every day, I was.

"I want you to work with one of my guys on this."

I was surprised to hear that. Usually if I did anything for the Chief it was in an *unofficial capacity.* And I always worked alone. I did things my way and got results. I wasn't bound by the usual constraints. Words like *due process* and *Miranda rights* had no place in my vocabulary. My old man played by the rules and I saw where that got him.

"Who you have in mind?" I asked.

"Ron Beachy."

Surprised, I asked, "Amish Ron?"

"The very same," Chief Caraway replied.

I told him that was fine. Said I was happy to help, but working this case with Detective Beachy was going to fuck everything up for me. Amish Ron was a legend in police work. He'd grown up Amish, but somewhere along the way he'd converted, became one of us. I supposed a man could only raise so many barns without growing jaded.

The parking lot was jam-packed tight when we arrived at Cowboy Roy's. It looked like a hundred people standing around, eating and drinking in the cold.

Big Tony and Doyle had plans; they'd do whatever it took to get the money. The word on the street was somebody got paid. Not enough to finance a revolution, but more than enough to kill for. If Telly was as dumb as he sounded, he was dead already.

I parked the Vic and enjoyed the beginnings of what was sure to be another outstanding drunk as I stood next to the Lincoln and waited for Big Tony to do another line of coke. He offered one to Doyle but Doyle never touched that shit. He didn't waste his time with drinking either, because it cut into too much of his time for stealing. When Doyle wasn't stealing, he was thinking about stealing. Or planning to steal something. He was the kind of guy who dreamed of stealing every night. And when Doyle couldn't sleep, he wouldn't count sheep—he stole them.

Even the watch on his wrist belonged to someone else, an established thief named Chuck Porter. He and Doyle went back to the days when Moses wore short pants and they had a rivalry of one-upmanship that was unmatched. They tried to out-steal the other in a friendly competition that Doyle eventually won when Chuck accidently got locked in a safe and ran out of air.

In a bold display of audacity, Doyle slipped the watch off Chuck's wrist at his funeral, while he was lying in the casket in front of everyone. Doyle'd been wearing it ever since.

I slammed the last of my Corona and threw the bottle in the dumpster. We passed people braving the cold. Drinking beer and eating chili.

Big Tony led the way through the doorway that not four hours earlier I'd stumbled out of. The same doorway where I'd passed that tweaker shit fuck Telly. *Goddammit.* If I'd only known. He probably had the money with him. Some detective I was.

Big Tony headed for his table and Doyle blazed a path to the shitter. Said it was the chili he ate earlier, the stuff they served in the parking lot.

I asked him about that.

"Every night in November," he said. "Gotta love Chili Month."

Indeed. As a man with a lifelong appreciation of strippers *and* chili, I found something extraordinary about the idea of combining them both under one roof. It was almost as if Cowboy Roy himself had created a Utopian Paradise to ensnare men for hours, separating them from their hard-earned dollars while giving them two of the greatest things life had to offer at the same time.

I waited for Flames to serve me up but a baby doll took my order instead. She was topless and wore a different-colored barbell through each pert nipple.

I asked her if that hurt.

"I didn't think about it." She turned away quickly. She thought herself too good for me and maybe she was. I watched the light reflect off her jewelry. Her face radiated nausea and revulsion. Without looking up, she asked me what I wanted.

"A shot of Patron. A shot of Jim Beam. A Corona. And a Captain n' Coke."

That finally got her attention. She wanted to complain but didn't. "Okay," she said.

She came back with the first two shots and I finished them both before she brought my beer. When she set the bottle on the bar, I grabbed the Captain from her hand and killed it too.

I held up a finger. Told her I wasn't done.

"*More?*"

"When it comes to drinking I don't fuck around." I threw a twenty on the counter, which wasn't nearly enough, and told her to set me up one more time.

I made an impressive dent in that Corona; I downed the Captain. Baby girl still hadn't come back with my next round.

To my right, a man wearing a polo shirt at least one size

too small looked over at me and licked the foam off his tremendous mustache. It was a serious mustache to be sure, a very powerful-looking Fu Manchu, grown with diligence and trimmed with precision. I could only begin to imagine the pride of ownership and the awesome responsibility associated with a mustache of that magnitude.

I wished baby doll would hurry up. Doyle and Big Tony were sitting at the table making plans without me. I had to get back there. They'd try and cut me out if I gave them the chance.

At the other end of the bar I could see her flirting with a younger guy who was much better-looking than me. He was also taller and wore an expensive suit. She worked that stud like a pro, pushing her plastic tits and aluminum hardware in his face.

I was ready for another drink but she dawdled, pursuing her own interests with little regard to my drinking schedule.

"Hurry the fuck up, babe," I snapped. Not loud enough to be heard over the music, but just loud enough to get the attention of Captain Mustache. He asked me if I had a problem.

"Of course I have a problem, *cockbreath! I wish this girl was on roller skates!*"

He stood quickly with a force that made his bar stool wobble. Then he gave me the silent treatment and let his mustache do the talking.

I didn't like the direction our conversation was taking. I knew I'd better act fast.

I handed him my beer suddenly and without warning.

"Here, hold this," I said as I shoved my beer into his palm, my voice brimming with authority.

His fingers close around the bottle automatically. Then he looked down at his hand for a moment, taking his eyes off of me as he wondered why the hell he was holding my Corona.

That's when I hit him in the throat with an open hand blow. I followed it with a quick right hook to the eye socket, then drove my knee into his nut bag for the takedown. Oddly enough he never dropped the bottle and I was able to grab it from his hand before he hit the floor.

Baby girl finally came back. This time she was yelling. She asked me what the fuck just happened.

"Call 911," I said. "This man just had a heart attack."

I finished my beer and downed the Patron. Then I gulped down the Beam and the Captain. I thanked her for the drinks and said her nipples were magnificent. Using the madness that ensued as cover I was able to retrieve my twenty from the bar without anyone noticing.

I rejoined the fellas at the table and wiped my bloody knuckles on the back of a fat guy I rubbed up against.

When I took my seat at the table, the conversation stopped abruptly. Big Tony's mouth was hanging open like the hinge on his jaw was broken and the weight of his teeth made it impossible to close.

"What the fuck was that?" He appeared stunned.

I took a drink and shrugged. I didn't know what he was talking about.

Doyle shook his head. "Get it together, man."

I assured both Doyle and Big Tony I was fine. I explained to them I was a highly functional alcoholic. I wasn't afraid to admit it. I'd come to terms with my curse long ago. I accepted it. Nobody had high expectations of a drunk and I used that to my advantage.

I finished the last of my Corona and set the bottle on the table a little too hard. "Let's talk," I said.

Big Tony had his box out and tapped it with his finger.

He looked around and I read his mind; he wanted another line but he was too lazy to go to the car. He'd have to wait for the right moment then break out his equipment.

Doyle leaned into the table and cracked his knuckles, ready to get down to business.

"Here's what we gotta do," he said. "We gotta follow his crew around, see what turns up."

"Parker's crew?" I asked.

"Yeah."

"We can do this," Big Tony chipped in.

Doyle was shaking his head in agreement. "It can't be that hard. Long as we stay on 'em, we'll find it. If they got it, that is." He sounded doubtful.

"What about the tweaker?" I asked. "We thinking he's dead?"

They both said that he must be dead, or would be soon. They had to be right. Even if Telly managed to still be alive, it was a safe bet he no longer had the cash. The fact that he failed to show up for his drug deal with Big Tony only confirmed our suspicions. Not that Big Tony came through on his end. He still never found any crank.

We talked for a while about Joe Parker and his crew.

Big Tony dumped a small mound of blow on his mirror as casually as anyone I'd ever seen. The fact we were surrounded by guys eating chili in a strip club didn't seem to bother him.

Doyle didn't like it, but as far as he could see Big Tony was getting away with it. "Hurry up and put that shit away," he said.

I took a bottle of Oxycontin from my pocket and looked for the closest waitress within shouting distance. I noticed that fuck with the handlebar mustache was gone but two of his buddies were giving me the smart eye. That was fine with me. But after a few more drinks I'd have something to say about it.

As I unscrewed the pill bottle, I looked up to find Doyle and Big Tony staring me down, both beaming out a gaze of disapproval.

"*What?*"

"Geez, Valentine," Big Tony said. "You're poppin' pills, too?"

I informed the degenerate thieves that I was going through a difficult period in my life and the medication was prescribed by my physician. I took two a day. And not because I was suffering from an injury of some kind, I just liked the way they made me feel. The temporary euphoria, short-lived though it may be, proved to be a fine companion to the liquor and coke.

Doyle sat back in his chair and crossed his arms. He played the role of caregiver and shot me a look of strong paternal disappointment.

Big Tony told me maybe I should slow down.

As much as I appreciated their concern, I found it absurd to get unsolicited counseling on substance abuse from a man about to snort cocaine. And I refused to be judged by anyone wearing the stolen watch of a dead man named Charlie.

Doyle stood up and walked to the bar. Told me he'd get me a beer.

"Thanks," I told him. "Grab me a Seven 'n' Seven while yer at it."

Big Tony sniffed a line of cocaine with a stealth that surprised me, then slid the mirror across the table. There wasn't enough there to get excited about, but I licked my finger and cleaned up what was left. I rubbed the inside of my mouth vigorously, then waited for the numbness to take hold.

I didn't have to wait long. That overwhelming lack of

sensation washed over my gums like a Novocaine dream as rap music blasted a ferocious assault. Vibrations from the mammoth speakers suspended from the ceiling caused my empty Corona to foxtrot across the table.

For a second everything felt right. Like the world was my slave and I had everything I needed.

Big Tony stopped a tall, thin dancer with long blonde pigtails who stood on enormous pink platform heels at least eight inches tall. Her body was tight and shaved clean. I watched her abdominal muscles flex and release under the cruel light of the single bulb that burned dimly above our beer-stained table.

She took Big Tony's drink order then asked me what I wanted.

I gave her a hard look and told her with my eyes.

She said I'd have to do better than that.

I sat up straight in my chair, my posture rigid and commanding.

I explained I had a skilled tongue that made women weep. Perhaps, under different circumstances, I could give her a demonstration. Then I asked her for a double shot of Maker's Mark, a Corona, and a shot of Cuervo Gold. Preferably with lime.

She walked away, bewildered.

Doyle returned and put the new Corona in my hand. He told me they were fresh out of Seagram's.

I told him not to worry as I dropped the next Oxy on my tongue. Doyle said he wasn't, then took a seat and told us what he'd come up with.

Parker's best man was a guy called English Sid. He asked me if I knew him.

I told him I thought so. That sounded like Parker's number one asshole.

Frank Sinatra in a Blender

"Uh huh, that's him," Doyle continued. "Well, I been thinkin'. Seems to me, we just gotta follow this English Sid. We follow him and he leads us to the money. Assuming he even has it. And assuming this tweaker fuck is even involved."

Doyle gave Big Tony a questioning look, but Big Tony was convinced.

"Telly's involved. He all but told me, the little shit."

"Yeah, I dunno." Doyle shrugged. "Just seems like you're still assumin' a lot."

Doyle was right. Big Tony was assuming a lot. But they didn't know about Norman Russo, a detail that could prove to be everything.

A few minutes passed without words as I continued to drink at a pace that would've made any competitive drinker proud. I finally broke the silence with a powerful belch and a brilliant idea.

"Let's just follow this cocksucker. We'll do it in shifts. Starting now."

I volunteered to go first, knowing full well I wouldn't have to.

Doyle clapped his hands together and leaned forward. "That's what I'm sayin'! If Parker's behind this, and he's probably behind this, then this English cocksucker's gotta be involved too. We follow him to the money."

Doyle offered to take the first watch just like I knew he would.

I understood Big Tony's bobbing head to mean he agreed. He was tapping his finger on the coke kit.

"It's our only move," I said. "But it still doesn't sound like much of a plan."

Doyle shrugged his shoulders and asked me if I could come up with anything better.

57

I drained the second half of my bottle and set the empty down gently this time. Told them I didn't know. There wasn't much to go on.

I failed to mention my involvement with the Chief. Thought some things were better left unsaid.

Before we could discuss things any further, the elegant blonde—the one I failed to enchant with empty promises and pornographic advances—returned in her monstrous pedestal shoes.

She set the tray down on the table and Big Tony grabbed his beer, told her to stick it on his tab.

Then she looked at me so I handed her a twenty and a ten. I thanked her for being perfect.

She met my stare when she took the money. Her eyes were gleaming bits of rough-cut jade in languid pools of lust. Everything about her mouth and throat was a warning. She made a perfect kiss with her *spank me* lips and marched out of my life, but she did the walk of shame to the stripper's pole with immeasurable grace.

Doyle seemed impressed. "I think maybe you could have her, Valentine."

I didn't say anything. Flawless moments like that didn't come often.

I hammered the first two shots and thought about a bowl of chili.

They spent the evening with most of Telly's body in the trunk of English Sid's car.

Mr. Parker said to cut him up. He wanted it done *his* way. He said to give Telly special treatment—his way of saying he wanted Telly cut up into eight individual pieces. The legs cut in half to make two pieces each. Each arm removed at the shoulder. The head separated from the torso.

Mr. Parker called that *The Eight Piece Deal*. It simplified the transportation of the limbs during the disposal process. But the prospect of sawing through muscle and bone for hours on end proved too difficult for them to even contemplate.

Sid had a better idea.

"Let's just chop his hands off, Johnny. Maybe his feet. We should probably cut his head off, too. Long as there's no fingerprints we'll be fine."

No Nuts agreed that was a better idea. A lot less messy too. Cutting and sawing through thigh and quadriceps muscle was hard work. But chopping off an ankle was a walk in the park.

They walked behind the church and grabbed an ax from an old shed they'd converted to a tool room, then they took bets on who could chop the feet off in the fewest blows.

They played *rock, paper, scissors* and No Nuts won, so he decided to let Sid go first.

Sid drew a mental line right above the ankle. He took a practice swing at half speed, stopped just shy of blade touching skin. Sid concentrated. Focused hard. There was five dollars riding on each swing.

Swoosh, his first attempt went clean through the bone and the ax plunked on the concrete. Sid began to smile.

"Not so fast, cocksucker," No Nuts said. "I don't think so."

"And why not?" Sid questioned. "The bloody blade went straight fuckin' through."

No Nuts squatted down, grabbed Telly's cold dead foot and leaned back with his weight. It started to give some; they could hear cold meat peeling away from the bone.

"Look, this fucker's still attached."

The exposed muscle was vivid and pink. There were muscle fibers still connecting everything together.

No Nuts accused Sid of being sloppy.

Sid said, "Okay, Johnny." Then he took another swing. This time there was no doubt. Telly's foot detached from his leg and Sid kicked it across the floor.

No Nuts smiled. "Not bad."

"Fuck you. That first one went clean through. I got jammed up on a bloody technicality."

"Uh-huh." Then, with no mental or physical preparation whatsoever, No Nuts took a powerful swing himself, using every ounce of energy his short, fat body possessed. But his aim was off and the brunt of the blow was absorbed by the concrete with a dull thud. The ax bounced out of Johnny's hands.

Sid laughed uncontrollably. He lost his balance, had to sit down.

No Nuts shook his head and finished with the legwork.

It was dark when they left the church. They spent the next three hours driving the St. Louis riverfront depositing limbs. They threw a leg in the Mississippi and an arm in the Missouri. No Nuts tossed a foot into a sewer in old St. Charles.

Sid took his time and drove the speed limit. He listened to bad music while No Nuts complained about the weather. About the price of gas. He complained about the Pope and he wasn't even Catholic.

They drove Interstate 270 to Highway 44. Most of the trip was spent in a heated debate over politics and healthcare. Sid asked No Nuts where he stood on abortion.

"It's a woman's choice," he said firmly.

Sid nodded. "Agreed. But, what about the baby, Johnny? Dontchya think that little bastard'd like to make up his own bloody mind before his whore of a mum goes and aborts him?"

"I thought you just said it was her choice?"

Sid raised his right palm, gave half a shrug. "I'm just sayin', Johnny."

No Nuts let that sit, but not for long. "So, you're sayin' if this broad you're seein' got knocked up you'd let her keep it?"

"I don't have a broad n'more, Johnny. We split up, remember?"

Sid missed the point entirely.

"Yeah, but what I'm sayin' is, if you still had some gal, and you knocked her up, would you tell her to get an abortion or let her keep it?"

"Oh, will you come on now, Johnny? We just chopped a man's bloody feet off, that's no kind of example to be settin' now is it?"

No Nuts looked out the window, tired of Sid pissing him off.

Sid looked over and smirked, said, "Besides, No Nuts, I got meself snipped a while back." Sid held up two fingers and made scissors. No Nuts held up one finger and told Sid to go fuck himself.

Their last stop was an access on the Meramec River in Fenton, just below the old Chrysler plant.

No Nuts told Sid, "I knew this guy, this bodybuilder, used to work at Chrysler."

Sid nodded, urged him to continue. "They built minivans, right? Well, I used to front him money for this thing he had goin' on. It was a helluva thing. They knew how them minivans went together, so they'd drive down to Mexico to buy steroids and sneak 'em back across the border inside these vans. Once they got home to Missouri, they'd go back to work, filling the interior body panels with steroids then shipping the vans off."

Sid was genuinely impressed at the blue-collar ingenuity of the autoworkers. "So where'd they send the gear to?"

"You know, different dealerships and shit. They hauled

'em on these transports; they'd know all the destinations beforehand. They tracked it all on computers and GPS. They kept it tight; only a few guys knew about it."

"That's pretty fucking spectacular, I'll say. How'd these blokes ever come up with such a thing?"

"Completely by accident."

Sid walked to the edge of the broken concrete slab and tossed an arm out into the river by the elbow.

"Go on, Johnny. How'd those cheeky bastards get a thing like this together?"

"That's what I asked my buddy. He said they met online, some bodybuilding site. One thing led to another, guess they started talkin', realized what they all done for a living. One guy worked at a dealership in Indiana, he knew a guy at a dealership in Virginia. Like social networking for drugs."

"But how'd they get the roids out of the vans?"

"That's the beauty of it Sid. These guys at the dealerships who were in on it'd take the vans apart soon as they got off the truck, then dole out the juice to their people. Then that guy'd take the 'roids to a gym, distribute to all the gym rats. Then BOOM, everybody buys uh couple bottles, they sell uh couple bottles, before long it spreads out like birdshot."

Sid told Johnny that was a hell of an idea. He asked him what happened to the plant.

"Greedy corporate cocksuckers. They run that place into the fuckin' ground." No Nuts spit a wad of solid yellow into a patch of mud as he walked to the very last speck of shore.

"Go on, punt it out there, Johnny."

No Nuts screwed his face down tight and pushed wrinkles together on his forehead. He lowered Telly's head out in front of him and dropkicked it. The wind took it and the head traveled high into the air before it hit the water.

Sid and No Nuts walked back to the Lexus as the snow

began to fall and pelted Sid's face. They got inside the neckline of his jacket and melted.

As they left the access road Sid cranked the heat and it warmed their faces. He yawned and stretched his neck to the side, happened to look down and saw Telly's dirty white tube sock with bright wet patches of blood showing through and staining the immaculate floorboard.

"Oh Johnny, ya wanker, you forgot the bloody teeth."

They'd smashed a few of Telly's teeth out with the hammer. No Nuts pulled out a few from the side with channel locks, but quickly abandoned the task after he got to the ones in the back.

"Them sumsbitches ain't coming out," he'd declared.

Now Sid looked down at his floorboard and told No Nuts he could fuck up a crowbar in a sandbox without bloody trying. Said he was gonna buy him a new floor mat.

"I'll throw 'em out the window, Sid."

"You do that, Johnny."

They drove under the Mraz U-turn exit as they passed the old minivan plant where a new Town & Country once perched high atop a platform in front of the complex. Now it was a lifeless carcass being demolished brick by brick. Sid told No Nuts that was too bad about Chrysler.

They left Fenton and blew past Hot Shots and the Stratford Inn, headed back to the city. No Nuts started complaining about the economy.

We finished our business, had a few more drinks, and did three more lines of coke. I took another Oxy. I was about as ruined as I'd ever been when I felt that familiar sense of total disorientation about to overpower me. I thought

I'd lost my keys. It didn't take long to realize I should've never taken that last Oxy.

Even I recognized it was time to go, and Nick Valentine was all about memorable exits. My system was operating on a monumental supply of alcohol and a Whitman's Sampler of chemicals, but at least I'd given up coffee.

I told the boys I'd see them tomorrow and bumped Big Tony's fist. I told that stripper with the pigtails and the platforms shoes she was the most amazing woman I'd ever seen in my life. And I let her know in no uncertain terms how much it would mean to me, on a personal level, if only I could take her back to the office and introduce her to Mr. Stout.

I yelled for Flames to have a good one, not even realizing I'd gotten this current drunk confused with my previous drunk. Then, with all the confidence and false sense of security that a good pharmaceutical high can offer, I yelled out for those guys at the end of the bar to go fuck themselves. I stumbled out the same door for the second time and walked right into the waiting arms of another topless dancer. But this one was holding a bowl of chili.

She was the skinniest girl I'd ever seen and her nipples were hard and sharp, like rigid tacks in the freezing air. If I *had* locked my keys in the Vic, I could've carried her to the car and turned her sideways. Used her nipples to cut through the glass and unlock the door. As thin as she was, I could've jammed her between the door and the window and used her skinny body as a Slim Jim.

She asked me if I wanted any chili.

"Fuck yes!" I grabbed the bowl from her hands and kept walking.

I found my keys hanging from the ignition, which meant I hadn't lost them. Which meant I wouldn't need to use that stripper's locksmith services after all.

When I pulled out onto Franklin Street, I punched the accelerator hard and made the rear tires spin across the intersection. I licked the plastic spoon clean and tossed it onto the passenger side floorboard along with the empty bowl. *Goddamn that was good chili.*

I only had one rule when it came to drinking. Don't eat while you're drinking.

There's nothing worse than fucking up a fifty-dollar beer buzz on a five-dollar hamburger, so I always kept the two separate. Like any good drunk should.

And as much as I enjoyed Oxy, one of the unfortunate drawbacks from painkillers was hunger. I hadn't eaten all day. I'd bought a pizza from the gas station but when I took it out of the mini to get the last ice cubes, I forgot to put it back.

As hungry as I was, I was not entirely opposed to the idea of eating a frozen pizza that had been thawing for five hours. But Frank Sinatra would have already gotten to it by now. In fact, I doubted he waited longer than it took for me to close the door.

In some ways, I envied Frank. His days were filled with eating, football fucking, and shit taking. He greeted each day on his own terms. You just had to admire that kind of philosophy.

I could see my destination looming in the distance—White Castle. Second only to Denny's as the restaurant of choice after a hard night of drinking, coke snorting, and pill popping.

I pulled into the drive-thru with nervous anticipation. I was about to play a dangerous game. I'd always considered myself a gambling man, but combining both chili and White Castle in the same sitting was like playing Russian Roulette with your asshole.

I ordered a crave case to go and a large Dr. Pepper and I shared my thoughts on *string theory vs. quantum mechanics* with the black gentleman at the window. I screeched out of the parking lot as more snow began to fall, and I went home to eat dinner with the only friend I had.

Ron Beachy grew up on a farm in Illinois, in Amish country. He had nine brothers and sisters and all of them worked from the earliest hints of morning light until the welcome darkness that late evening brought. He never liked that life. Nor did he support the idea of a life spent foregoing simple things everyone else in the world took for granted. Like electricity.

Ron was a firm believer that some things were just worth having. Even from an early age he could see there was life beyond the tree line that separated his county from the next. At night he'd see the lights on the horizon, blazing through the pitch-black darkness with a cornucopia of swirling colors. The thought of crossing that line became a goal when he was twelve and his father forced him to set up his own cabinet shop.

Little Ronnie was up by five every morning, out in his shop ten minutes later. He'd start working on the pieces he'd stained the night before. His tools were a hammer, a tape measure, and a box of finishing nails. He'd work in the shop until dusk. Then he'd go out to the woods at first light the next morning to check the traps he'd set the night before.

He'd bring whatever opossum, squirrel, coon, or coyote he trapped back to the shop and turn them loose. Let them run all day in his cabinet shop until he got home from school. Then he'd kill them and skin them out.

After breakfast, the Beachy children would arrive at school by horse and buggy. His older brother David would operate the reins. This was the pattern his life took until the day he turned eighteen, when he left home with a trashbag full of clothes and three hundred dollars. He walked to the county line and as the sun came up he took the steps he had waited so long to take.

Then he crossed into a world of brutal violence. A world where men murdered other men because they didn't like their haircut. He joined the Police Academy and his first job was Deputy Sheriff of a small town in Franklin County. With a population of a couple of thousand, it was a place to start, but Ron missed the excitement that he'd found in the big city. He'd been to the racetrack, the casinos, and nightclubs.

The city was a brave new world to explore and he greeted each day as a new adventure. There were suicides, homicides, drive-by shootings. Ron Beachy buried himself in police-work. He immersed himself in crime scene reconstruction until he was the expert that other cops went to when they needed answers.

Ron became known for his unconventional methods, and he was a pioneer with a natural ability to view each situation through cleaner, unspoiled eyes. He had superior instincts and a strong moral compass. He was a creative thinker and a visionary in the field with a solid reputation as the most highly accomplished detective in St. Louis. That's why Chief Caraway assigned Ron Beachy to the credit union case.

Sid picked up Johnny No Nuts at his house in Sunset Hills. They slid all over the street in the fresh snow that fell the night before. It didn't amount to much but it was just enough to fuck everything up as far as driving went. No Nuts was voicing his opinion by the end of the road.

"Why we gotta get the tweaker's car?"

"Aw, c'mon, Johnny." Sid didn't want to hear him complain about anything. At least not until he had his breakfast. They had a rule. No Nuts could bitch about whatever he wanted. Long as Sid got a chance to eat something first.

"Sid, I'm just askin'. Why we gotta get this fuck's car? It ain't like he'll be needin' it."

Mr. Parker told Sid they had to get Telly's car. Told him they should park it down in the city and let the niggers steal it.

"We should take it down to Kinloch," Johnny said. "Won't last ten minutes in Kinloch."

The last time Sid heard mention of Kinloch, a man in a wheelchair had gotten robbed and set on fire. People drove by as he burned alive and nobody helped. The crime rate was towering; people down there would steal anything. Sid told No Nuts he was right. "If it's not welded to the floor they'll take it."

The road to Montgomery's was an obstacle course of cars in ditches, tow trucks in the emergency lane, and snow plows barreling through it all.

They finally pulled up behind Telly's shitbox and Sid told No Nuts to jump behind the wheel, follow him down to the city. No Nuts said he would, but he made it as far as the driver's seat before he turned around and came back.

"What's the problem, Johnny? If your legs ain't long enough to reach the pedals you can scoot that seat up."

"Fuck you," No Nuts said. "There ain't no keys."

"What?" Sid demanded.

"Guess he took 'em out of the ignition."

Sid closed his eyes. "*Fuck.*" He leaned back in the seat.

No Nuts shrugged. "Sorry, Sid."

The keys were in Telly's pants. Now that he thought about it, Sid remembered seeing them. He'd checked Telly's pockets himself. It just never occurred to him they'd need them. He didn't know Mr. Parker'd want the car moved. He wasn't a mindreader.

Still, if No Nuts felt the need to accept responsibility, Sid would certainly allow him to take the blame.

"That's okay, Johnny."

They sat there for a minute as Sid contemplated their next move. He was doing the thinking for the both of them. On a whim, Sid looked over at Johnny. Asked him, "You ever check the trunk?"

Johnny scratched his head, said, "No."

"Well, why don't you go and check it out then, Johnny. Y'know, just in case."

No Nuts gave Sid a *fuck you* look as he got out of the warm car. He walked back to the driver's side and climbed in. A few seconds later the trunk popped open and No Nuts walked around to the back.

When he saw the duffel bag, No Nuts froze. His feet slipped in the snow, and he went down on his ass. He stood up, tried it again. Grabbed the open trunk lid to hold himself in place. His heart started drumming up against his ribs.

What the fuck was this?

I woke up on the couch in an awkward position. I couldn't remember going to bed. I couldn't remember much about last night at all. I remembered Cowboy Roy's and something about nipples, but the rest was a blur. I'd be sure to do a visual inspection of the Vic before I began the new day. The condition of my car was a pretty accurate gauge of the destructive events that may or may not have occurred the night before.

I rolled over on my side and saw empty White Castle boxes scattered across the floor. That's right, White Castle. Frank and I must have thrown down the party gauntlet before I passed out.

I tried to sit up but my head was throbbing like there was a midget inside my skull smashing everything he could reach with a sledgehammer. Frank was lying on the floor beside me, licking his testicles. The way he was going to town you'd think he was trying to shine them.

"You make that look so easy," I told him, but he never looked up. Frank was too busy taking care of whatever business he was taking care of. I stumbled through the kitchen, told Frank he walked a fine line between self-cleaning and self-gratification. Undaunted, he continued with the task at hand.

I needed an ice-cold Mountain Dew. It was the best cure for a hangover I knew. But first I'd grab a shower and knock some of my funk off. Then I'd need to find a toothbrush. At some point a powerful shit was in order, especially taking into account my recent attempt to undermine my digestive system.

My phone rang before I could make my next move and I spent the next ten minutes talking with Detective Beachy. I asked him what he had in mind.

"Let's meet and talk this over."

"Sure, name the place."

"How 'bout that little breakfast joint off Howdershell? Rosebud's? You know the place?"

"Lemme get this straight, Ron. You wanna meet at a pancake shop?"

Ron laughed. Said they had the best French toast in the world.

I told him I knew the place and that was fine by me. I asked him if they had Mountain Dew.

He laughed some more, told me they had great coffee. The coffee was even better than the French toast. He asked me what I thought about that.

I told Ron, I hated it. I'd given up coffee some time ago; I'd appreciate it if he didn't bring it up again.

Ron didn't know what to say so he laughed. Told me he'd buy me a pancake.

I said I'd see him soon.

An hour later, I was on the road. Running late and driving much too fast for conditions. It was ten in the morning and the window was down a crack, just enough to let the ice-cold wind blow against my face while I drove. I would have left sooner, but Frank refused to shit in the snow. After much coaxing and many threats, he finally took a dump underneath the Vic on the only patch of dry land he could find. I should have just let him shit on a magazine like he usually did but I wanted him to experience the awe of nature.

I pulled into Rosebud's almost twenty minutes late. On one hand it seemed too early for a drink but on the other hand I was ready. I found Amish Ron behind the table with a book in his hand called *Conspiracy Theories for Dummies*. I had to laugh.

Detective Beachy stood up and offered a proper greeting. "Hey, Nick." He nodded and gave me a firm, genuine handshake. He looked me in the eye and told me I looked good. Asked what I'd been up to.

He'd gained a few pounds since the last time I'd seen him but looked damn good for a man in his late forties. His hair was salt and pepper. He had a strong chin and good, even teeth with a confident smile. He laughed at everything. Combined with his slight Dutch accent, he had a natural charisma that immediately put you at ease. But Ron was a master of subterfuge—a valuable asset for interrogations.

71

Every question was part of a chess game, and he had all the answers. Ron told me he was training for the bomb squad. A technician spot was coming up and he meant to take it.

I told him he'd make a good one. His attention to detail was second to none.

Ron didn't waste any time. He asked about my drinking.

I told him it was going pretty well. I thought I'd finally found something I was good at.

This insight brought forth a great laugh that warned me I'd be under surveillance from that point on. It was Ron's way of letting me know we could have a problem if I wasn't careful. The Chief must've told him to keep his eye on me.

I ordered breakfast and pulled a bottle from my pocket. I twisted the top off and let the carbonated fluid donkey punch my taste buds with the refreshing burn that only a cold Mountain Dew could provide. It was medicinal and it was what I needed to survive.

Ron asked me if I'd had a hard night.

I told him every night was a hard night on the streets of St. Louis.

The conversation began to flourish from that point. One thing led to another, and before long we were making progress on the credit union case.

The credit union wasn't releasing any information about the money. "All they're saying's there was an incident and a shooting," Ron said.

"*An incident?* Somebody robbed them in a bread truck."

Ron shrugged. "Well they ain't saying much, but I think they got hit hard. They had a big currency drop the night before with everybody's Christmas Club money coming due. Sounds like whoever hit the credit union knew about that money."

It sounded to me like they were just waiting to see what

went down on the street. Let the pressure build. Let people talk. Somebody'd feel the need to stroke his own ego before long. A criminal's worst enemy was himself.

I asked him what else he knew. Told him not to bullshit me either, we were a team. I didn't expect to be left out of any part of this investigation and wanted full disclosure.

"Don't leave anything out," I said.

Detective Beachy took a big bite of English muffin that left a smear of butter at the corner of his mouth, something that bothered me right away but I let go of.

"Is there anything you're not tellin' me, Nick?"

"Me? C'mon Ron. What do I know?"

He took another bite of muffin and grinned. If that patch of butter didn't come off with the next sip of coffee I'd have to say something.

"You've got ears on the street," Ron said.

"Which is exactly why you need me."

Ron finally took that drink of coffee but he stopped grinning. He brought the cup back to the table and dabbed his mouth, somehow missing the butter altogether.

"Ron," I said as I dabbed at the corner of my own mouth with a napkin and nodded towards him.

The smiled returned to his face. "Oh." He wiped his lip clean. "That bothered you, didn't it?"

It must've been some kind of a test. *Goddamn that Amishman.*

"Not at all," I said. "I just wanted you to know you could trust me. Wouldn't want you to walk around all day with butter on your face and look like an asshole."

A bearded man with suspenders walked up to the table and poured Ron another cup of coffee; not a word was said between them. When he walked off, I told Ron something wasn't right about that guy.

Ron laughed deeply, put his hand on his belly. Said I was a better detective than he thought.

"Why? What's wrong with him?"

He couldn't quit laughing long enough to tell me the story. He started twice, but couldn't keep it together. He took a deep breath, told me he'd need a cigarette for this and he pulled one from his pack.

"*You can't smoke in here!*" I said. It was bad enough I had to watch the bastard drink coffee. A smoke was more than I could tolerate without suffering a breakdown. I simply wasn't strong enough. The only alternative I could think of was a cold beer to rebuild my strength.

He lit up a Winston anyway. Said, "Fuck Rosebud, I'll do what I want."

"That's Rosebud?"

"That's Rosebud."

Ron held his finger up, took another breath. Said, " 'Bout a year ago we busted this lady with a little dope, right? Older gal, pulled her over for speedin'. They take her in, go through her bag. They find a few DVDs, right?"

I shrugged, not sure where this was going.

"Well, she had a video of her fucking a German Shepard. Another one of her blowing a Dalmatian. Fucked-up shit. A video of some guy pissing on her foot." With that, he lost his ability to continue with the story.

"Christ! Are you shitting me, Ron?"

He couldn't take it anymore. He set that Winston down on his plate, caught up in a fit of laughter beyond his control.

I knew we were living in a fucked-up world, but still.

Detective Beachy regained control and picked up his Winston. He took a deep drag and blew a mouthful of stale air up toward the ceiling. He asked me if I was ready.

"I'm ready when you are." I stood up, started digging

ones from my pocket. Ron reached down and touched my arm, told me not to worry.

I thanked him, said that was nice.

"Don't thank me."

He told me I should thank Rosebud. Said he never paid for breakfast here on account of that gal on those videos was Rosebud's sister.

"Don't tell me this son-of-bitch knew about her acting career?"

"You could hear his voice in the background, Nick. I was thoroughly disgusted."

We walked out of Rosebud's and I felt like depositing the contents of my stomach in the parking lot. There were Internet sites that paid good money for that kind of thing, but I didn't understand the appeal. No matter how much I tried to distance myself from the thought, I couldn't believe the guy who'd just made my pancakes could film his own sister blowing a Dalmatian.

In my mind I vowed never to return. But there was another part of me, a hungrier part of me, which thought about a future with free breakfast now that I knew Rosebud's secret. I could stop by for lunch, too. Before long I'd be having all my meals there. But still, my image of the Fireman's Best Friend was forever tainted.

Doyle was sitting in front of the Indigo Building a half hour before the sun came up. He couldn't sleep. He was too excited about the job. He'd already been eyeballing the building for a couple of weeks, trying to get a feel for who was who. Doyle watched the comings and goings of its occupants around the clock.

After a while he learned who wasn't worth remembering and who was worth looking into. A man named Joe Parker had been worth looking into.

Joe Parker was a businessman. He owned a construction company, a moving company, and an auto body shop. He also ran a crew that was responsible for half the sex, drugs, and firearms that found their way into St. Louis. Parker was connected but he was smart enough not to get his hands dirty.

Parker was a perfect candidate, so Doyle learned his schedule. Always predictable, Parker left for work by eight and was home by five. On Wednesday nights he bowled; out of the house by six, back home at eleven. He was always loud and frequently drunk.

His wife had a variety of hobbies herself and plenty of reasons to stay away. Doyle never saw her much, but when he did she was always flashing diamonds.

They were the perfect couple.

When Big Tony mentioned the news about the tweaker's possible involvement with Joe Parker, Doyle got his hopes up. He didn't tell him he'd already been casing Parker's building. He didn't tell him he already had plans to rob him.

The word on the street from the people who knew was maybe something big had just gone down. Doyle was ready.

He waited until nine in the morning when English Sid pulled up in his Lexus and went inside. Twenty minutes later, Doyle was behind him. He watched Sid pick up No Nuts, and he followed them to breakfast. He followed them to Montgomery's. He was watching when No Nuts pulled the duffel bag from the trunk of what he could only assume was the tweaker's car. Doyle watched the fat fuck fall down in the snow, but he was too worked up to laugh.

Those cocksuckers actually had the money.

Sid was slapping No Nuts on the shoulder as he pulled away from the parking lot. Laughing because Johnny fell in the snow. Laughing because he was drunk with thoughts of power. There was enough money in the bag to escape. He could put a bullet in Johnny's head and disappear without a trace.

But he never considered it. Sid was Mr. Parker's right-hand man, and he knew a thing or two about loyalty.

No Nuts, on the other hand, *was* dumb enough to run, but smart enough to know he'd never make it on his own.

"How much money you reckon's back there, Johnny?" Sid gestured toward the duffel bag in the trunk with the back of his head.

Johnny's eyebrows arched up; he looked serious. "Millions, Sid. Millions."

Sid was still smiling; now he laughed. "*Millions?*"

"Fuck yeah, dontchya think?"

Sid shrugged. Stuck his bottom lip out, said, "Hell if I know. But I don't think you could fit that much money in the bag, Johnny."

Johnny assured him that you could. "That's a big bag, Sid. It'll hold millions, trust me." No Nuts spoke with the authority of a man who was an expert on such things.

The Lexus bounced through a pothole, and the tires broke traction in the slush. They thought the best place to stash the money was at Parker's. Sid had a key. They headed back to the Indigo Building with Doyle two car links behind them.

Big Tony stepped out of the shower and ran a comb through his disheveled mop. He heard his cell phone ringing in the bedroom but ignored it. He didn't get much sleep on account of the coke, and he didn't feel like talking. He left Cowboy Roy's alone, again. He'd let another one of those vixens play him for a fool. They'd rubbed their vaginas against his knee and talked him out of drinks. Talked him out of lines. Despite his Herculean efforts, he'd yet to bring one home.

Once again his phone rang, and he saw that it was Doyle. "Yeah, what up?"

"What up? We just might be rich ya big bastard, that's what's up."

Big Tony said nothing.

"Hey, you there?" Doyle was excited, talking fast.

"Slow down, slow down. What's going on?"

"Tony, I think they got the money, man. Looks like it, anyway."

"Wha?" His mouth dropped open. Big Tony had almost forgotten about the money; hadn't thought about it all morning.

"I am not shitting you, man. Pretty sure I just saw it."

Big Tony sat down on the edge of his bed. He asked Doyle if he was serious.

Doyle laughed. "Fuck yes I'm serious you cocksucker! Now get dressed and meet me downtown."

Doyle gave him the address. Told him about following Sid and No Nuts. He told him how he'd already been staking out Joe Parker's building for a while now, how he'd planned on robbing him anyway.

"I already got the whole layout of the Indigo, Tony. I got it all."

"*I'm rich,*" Big Tony said to himself. He couldn't believe this was happening.

"*I'm rich.*" Big Tony said again, louder this time. "We're both rich, Doyle!"

Doyle was grinning and switching lanes. His car slid around in the snow.

"We ain't rich yet so calm down, man. Get a hold of yourself and meet me at the club. I gotta stick with these guys. Call me back in an hour, we may roll today."

They both hung up and focused on managing their business.

I left Rosebud's with strict intentions of not returning for at least a week. I followed Ron to Norman Russo's house so he could check things out for himself. He asked me if that was all right with me.

I told him it was. Said we had to start somewhere. Besides, he may as well have a look himself. I was interested to see if our theories aligned.

We parked our cars and met at the end of the driveway. Ron looked over at the Vic.

"Is that police issue? I've never seen a black one."

"*Was,*" I told him.

"Really?"

The Vic was blacker than a woodchuck's asshole at midnight, with tinted windows and a chrome spotlight mounted to each mirror. It rumbled when you hit the key, courtesy of the foot-long glass packs that funneled the exhaust out through three-inch stainless steel pipes.

Ron looked at me and paused, his way of letting me know he was about to ask me something I'd have to lie about.

"Did'ya take the shotgun out?"

I assured him I had, in fact, removed the shotgun. I didn't tell him I replaced it with another shotgun—a 12-gauge short-barrel pump-action with a pistol grip—or that I had a Stihl chainsaw in the trunk.

We opened the front door using a key Ron had. Everything looked as it did the night before. We got to the steps, and he began to shake his head. "He picked a bad place to hang himself," he said. "What do you think?"

"Couldn't've picked a worse place if he'd tried."

Ron looked up at the ceiling and the walls. "We can agree on that."

He pulled a clear baggie from the inside of his suit jacket and handed it to me.

"What do you make of this?"

I told him I recognized it from the night before. It was that suicide note, written by someone with the grammar skills of a third-grader.

He nodded. "Pretty obvious this isn't his handwriting."

I dealt the Amishman exaggerated sarcasm. "You mean Norm didn't write that note himself?"

Ron shook his head. Said he couldn't believe this shit. "Is anybody really that stupid?"

Ron flipped through a notebook. "According to Mr. Russo's attorney, he and his wife were fighting over the house, but that's tough to swallow as a motive for suicide."

"He was already dead if you ask me. I think somebody broke his neck then tried to make it look like a hanging." I could tell Ron agreed. "Not to mention only an asshole would try'n hang himself from that old two-by-four and expect it to support his weight."

Ron walked down to the bottom of the stairs. "So we're supposed to believe he hangs long enough to, what, choke? Then the rope breaks, or the board pulls loose, whatever happens first. And then his lifeless body just tumbles to the bottom step."

"That's the evidence someone tried to manufacture, yes."

"Someone didn't think this through."

I walked over to the fridge because you could tell a lot about a man from the contents of his refrigerator. I started looking through containers for money, knowing smart people keep their money in the fridge. That's where I kept mine.

I found a half-gallon of milk, the usual assortment of condiments, lunchmeat, half a bottle of wine. My eyes locked onto the wine bottle, and before I could stop myself I was pulling out the cork, letting the Chardonnay fill my mouth.

I finished off the bottle, refilled it with tap water, and returned it to the fridge. I saw another bottle of wine on the top shelf over the sink.

"Find anything up there, Nick?"

"*Uh, no.* Not yet. Still looking, Ron."

The other bottle was an older Cabernet Sauvignon, by far my red wine of choice if I were selective. It looked expensive and would never be missed, but sadly I noted it would not fit in the pocket of my trousers. I walked around to the sliding glass door and unlocked it. I knew I'd be coming right back to have another look around and could pick up that fine bottle when I did.

Ron stomped up the stairs and looked around the kitchen. "You find anything?"

"Looks like somebody just went shopping." I pointed to the refrigerator. "Kind of an odd thing to do just before you kill yourself, dontchya think?"

Ron shook his head, told me I was right. He peered into

the empty trashcan, but the trash had already been collected by technicians and bagged for evidence .

I stepped into the garage. It was spotless. There was a Harley-Davidson in the corner that looked like it had never been ridden, a full dresser with hard bags and screaming eagle pipes, a few tennis rackets hung on the wall, plus a rake and a snow shovel. Both clean and unused.

I opened the door to a new Range Rover and hit the key. Only 11,468 miles and a full tank of gas.

I rummaged through the console and found a money clip with six twenties and a few tens. I knew if those incompetent rookies would've checked the garage, they'd have bagged the money as evidence or stolen it like I was about to do. I slipped it in my pocket and the metal was cold against my leg.

I closed the door to find Ron standing behind me.

"Find what you're looking for?"

Though startled, I didn't miss a beat. "He had a full tank of gas. Looks like he filled up about thirty-one miles ago."

"A full tank, huh?"

"A full tank," I confirmed.

"Okay," Ron began, "so this guy, this banker, he gets off work, he buys groceries, tops off his tank, then he goes home and hangs himself above his stairs?"

"And he ties the rope around a board so thin I could break the wood in half with my cock."

Amish Ron burst into spontaneous, unprompted laughter that echoed in the garage.

When he stopped laughing, he told me this was now officially a homicide. Said they could use a guy like me back on the force. Mentioned I was smart.

He didn't mention the stolen money in my pocket and I wondered if he'd seen it.

"One of these days," I told him. But I thought about that

wine in the kitchen. I planned on coming back to pick that up as soon as I lost Amish Ron. I'd have another look around too. Probably pay a visit to the shitter. The remnants of last night's ravenous suicide mission tumbled around violently in my guts.

We walked back into the kitchen; Ron stopped and relocked the sliding door. He shook his head. "Fucking amateurs," he said, referring to the cops from last night. The same cops who failed to process the garage with any real degree of professionalism.

No wonder the Chief was always calling me.

I followed Amish Ron back out the front door, teeth clenched in frustration. Ron was a happy-go-lucky rocket scientist with the curiosity of a five-year-old and uncanny powers of observation.

"I'm headin' back to the station, Nick."

I told him I had to run back to my office and take care of Frank, said I'd meet up with him later. I jumped in the Vic before he could protest.

B ig Tony pulled out of Cowboy Roy's with Doyle in the passenger seat telling him what he knew. Said he'd followed English Sid and that other idiot back to the Indigo Building, but they pulled into the parking garage and blocked his view. By the time Doyle got out of the car, Sid's Lexus was pulling back out.

Doyle ran back to his car and chased them down, followed them to Mr. Parker's construction business. He watched them get out of the Lexus and go inside, but they never took the bag from the trunk.

"What're you sayin'?" Big Tony asked.

"I'm sayin' I think the bag's in Parker's condo."

"You think?"

Doyle said it was either that or it was still in the trunk of the Lexus.

Big Tony hit a red light and came to a stop; the tires on the Lincoln locked up and slid for about a foot.

"So I guess we're goin' to the Indigo?"

"We're goin' to the van first, then *I'm* goin' to the Indigo. I don't need you gettin' in the way and stopping' every five minutes to do coke."

Big Tony licked his lips. He was already thinking about it. If only he could persuade Doyle to chop him out a line while he manhandled the Town Car through this slush. He'd stopped at his dealers and got an eight ball of premium cocaine. Way beyond his price range for three-and-a-half grams under normal circumstances, but in light of recent events he felt the need to indulge in something exceptional.

Doyle rolled his eyes when Big Tony started dicking with the radio.

"Go!" Doyle yelled, when the light turned green.

He made a right and found a station with some talk radio. The disc jockey was counseling a caller who had issues with his father. He told the D.J. his father never loved him because he always gave him poor advice.

"This guy's a peckerhead," Doyle said.

"Fucking crybaby," Big Tony added.

They listened in silence until the first commercial break, then Big Tony turned it down.

"Your old man pretty good with advice?"

Doyle chuckled. "Fuck no. He was either locked down or he was drunk." Doyle paused and reflected. He hadn't thought about his old man in a long time. "Either way, he wasn't big on advice as I recall."

"So you feel like this guy on the radio?"

Doyle laughed, told him this guy was an asshole. He looked out the window and cracked his knuckles as Big Tony surfed through the stations yet again.

Doyle had a good chuckle, more to himself than anything. "I think I can only remember that son-of-a-bitch givin' me one bit of advice before he died."

Big Tony looked over at Doyle. "Yeah, what was that?"

"Never wear sweatpants to a strip club."

"Huh?"

"That's what he said."

"That's the best advice your old man ever gave you?"

Doyle shrugged. "That's it."

The fat man behind the wheel began to laugh.

Doyle looked over from the passenger seat. "What?"

"That's just funny, is all."

"Yeah, well what's the best advice your old man ever gave you?"

"Only advice he ever give me was with his belt."

"Yeah, but that makes sense about the sweat pants if you think about it." Doyle reached over and turned off the radio when Rush Limbaugh came on. "I hate that asshole."

"He's okay," Big Tony countered.

They drove in silence for a couple of minutes until they hit traffic. They were stopped next to road construction and the guy on Doyle's side was working a jackhammer. Doyle put his window up all the way and checked his stolen watch.

"We got plenty of time," Big Tony said.

Doyle knew what time it was; he just didn't want to be late, and didn't want to end up listening to Rush the whole time.

They found the parking garage with no problems. Big Tony parked next to the van at the end of the aisle and Doyle stepped out.

"You stay close, case I need ya."

Big Tony said he would; he let his foot off the brake and the car started to roll.

"Good luck," he yelled, as Doyle slammed the car door, then unlocked the driver's side door of the van.

He climbed into the seat then turned and made a quick inventory of his equipment. Everything he needed was in an oversize hockey bag. A high-speed drill, two sledgehammers, chisels, hacksaws, an oxyacetylene torch, asbestos gloves, and a portable hydraulic jack. *Doyle was prepared.* When it came to a job he left nothing to chance.

He let the van warm up in the garage as he studied the floor plan to the building. The floor plan he was clever enough to procure a month ago. Getting it was the easy part. He found a unit for sale then went to the real estate agent as the concerned son of a perspective buyer.

"I'm looking for something for my parents, you see. Getting up there in years you know. *How's the Security?*"

It worked, like it always did, and they gave him all the information he required, including the floor plan.

Doyle left the garage and fell in with the bulky, concentrated flow of traffic as he made his way to the heart of the *Loop*. He passed the Tivoli Theater, then Meshuggah Coffee House on his left. He sat for a minute in front of the Delmar Lounge while a group of girls in bright-colored jackets sloshed across the street in the snow, their matching scarves blowing in the wind. He made a few turns, then pulled into the parking garage of the Indigo building.

I got back to my office just before the sun went down. It was colder than a well digger's ass in January and I drove like a maniac considering the road conditions. Amish Ron fucked me good when he noticed that back door unlocked. I'd planned on returning within minutes and doing a much more comprehensive search. Right after I drank that Cabernet Sauvignon and took a shit in Norm Russo's toilet.

I climbed the stairs two at a time with a respectable stride that even Frank would've envied. I slammed my key in the lock, hit the handle, and kicked the bottom of the door open with my foot.

Frank was sleeping in my office chair when I burst across the room, stumbled over a basket of dirty clothes, and knocked a box over. Frank started barking when everything spilled out onto the floor, but he directed his anger specifically at an oversized yellow plastic blender that bounced across the tile.

"*Rarp, rarp, arp!*"

I kicked the bathroom door so hard the wood popped and splintered at the top around the antique hinge. My pants hit the floor and my ass made contact with the seat without a moment to spare. As much as I'd enjoyed those White Castle sliders, I knew sooner or later I was bound to pay the price for the renegade behavior I'd so irresponsibly demonstrated the night before.

Relentless, Frank barked the whole time I was in the bathroom.

"Okay," I yelled as I walked from the john. "What the hell's your problem, Frank?"

He danced around in front of the door. Then he raced to the blender and barked. He took turns doing that over and over while I buttoned up my pants and drew my belt tight.

When I asked him if he had to go, Frank got excited. He snorted several times, turned two complete circles, then did a burnout across the tile and bounced off the door.

I told him I'd be right with him. I had to collect my thoughts after such a brutal, unforgiving shit. *Never again*, I swore. I hoped White Castle burned to the ground.

Frank was going crazy. Barking, doing donuts. Scratching the hell out of the bottom six inches of the back of my door.

"I'm coming." I picked Frank up and carried him down to the alley, where I was confident he'd piss on as many things as he possibly could as long as it didn't involve stepping in snow.

When we reached the sidewalk Frank did not disappoint me. He made it only two feet before he pissed on the welcome mat. Then he hiked his leg on a McDonald's cup. He looked around curiously. Sniffed and snorted. He ran over to a concrete step and moved his bowels underneath a faded green campaign sign that was still stuck in the ground a year and a half after the election.

He finished up with a world-record eight more pisses then he ran the Firecracker 500 up the stairs and waited for me by the door. When I got upstairs, I walked to my desk and grabbed a bottle of Southern Comfort, mixed a splash with some orange juice. I needed a few more So Co's to get my head in the game. I rummaged through the junk drawer on my desk and found a Vicodin that looked tempting. I dropped it down the hatch and watched Frank chew on his ass while the Chairman of the Board sang quietly in the background. Outside the frost-glazed window snow flurries did ballet in the arctic winter air.

Doyle rolled into the parking garage in a van that said Naramore Locksmith Co. and parked by the elevator. He set a few orange cones outside the van. If there was one thing he'd learned in the thieving business, the most important tools you could ever have on a job were orange cones. People accepted orange cones, never questioned them. Placing them around a commercial van parked in a handicap slot added just the right touch of legitimacy.

He removed the hockey bag with effort and slung the strap over his shoulder. He moved toward the elevator with a wig covering most of the right side of his face, the side the security camera would film. He held a handkerchief in his right hand and used it to push buttons and open doors. Doyle dropped the bag onto the floor to give his shoulder a rest as the elevator began going up.

Once Doyle decided to hit Mr. Parker, he did what he always did. He wrote a letter to the lock firm on letterhead that *he* printed up, and they pretty much gave him anything he asked for. In this case: the master keys. Doyle had everything he needed for the job; he'd planned it meticulously; he'd left nothing to chance.

When the elevator opened, he stepped into the lavish hallway of the Indigo and walked carefully to Apartment 202. He knocked loudly to be sure no one was home before he slid his master key into the lock. From previous surveillance, he already knew there was a dead bolt, but he wasn't worried.

Everybody had a deadbolt, but nobody used it.

He heard the tumblers move, and *click*. He suddenly found himself inside the living room, and he closed the door slowly, quietly. Then he got that funny taste in his mouth, the taste only a home invader would know and appreciate. Short of climaxing inside one of Cowboy Roy's girls, it was the greatest moment he would ever know.

Doyle made a visual inspection of the apartment to guarantee he was alone. Once Doyle was satisfied, he set his bag on the kitchen table, walked quickly to the bedroom. He found several pairs of earrings on the nightstand, then a necklace. He dropped them in a little pilfer bag he wore around his waist, along with several rings. Next he pulled open the wife's top dresser drawer and found some more loose jewelry, lipstick, and perhaps the best find of all, a gigantic purple dildo. It had a face at one end and a little set of feet at the other. He dropped that in the bag for laughs.

More jewels in the bathroom and a damn expensive watch. Doyle picked up a choice pair of cufflinks as well, then made his way to the closet. That's where the safe was. That's *always* where the safe was.

Except this time it wasn't.

Doyle'd spent a lot of time studying the floor plan to the unit so he found the safe in the bathroom on his second guess. Before he went to retrieve his bag from the kitchen he checked the door, just in case. Sometimes the kind of people who installed deadbolts and didn't use them were the same kind of people who didn't lock their safe. The Parker's were lazy and complacent. The door came open with a click.

Doyle swallowed hard, his palms sweating through his gloves.

He pulled the big door open to find papers, envelopes, folders, and loose cash. Maybe five, six thousand. *Fuck!* He started thinking. The bag was too big to fit in the safe anyway. He'd been so consumed by the thought of breaking in the Indigo and walking out with the money he failed to consider the raw facts.

It was always the little things that could make or break a job.

Doyle closed the door without taking any money. He couldn't risk tipping their hand. He couldn't risk Parker knowing they were onto him. His stopwatch beeped; he was running out of time. Doyle sprinted back to the bedroom, started putting things back. Suddenly everything felt wrong and his cheeks were burning. Instinct told him to run, but where was the money?

He only lost sight of them for a few minutes. How many minutes? Ten? Fifteen?

Doyle started looking around the room. Under the bed, behind closed doors. It must have been in the trunk of the car. He called Big Tony, but he got no answer.

Doyle walked back to the living room and thought. He paced, he went over everything in his head and then suddenly the pieces clicked together like math. If he were the Englishman, he'd keep the money.

Suddenly Doyle knew. Those fucks decided to keep it for themselves. He thought about the scene from Montgomery's. He'd seen them find the money and they'd been surprised. It was still early, the police weren't saying much. Parker didn't know the heist had gone down, assumed the deal was dead.

So the Englishman killed the tweaker without realizing he had the money in the trunk of his car.

The top of Doyle's cheeks dimpled with a mischievous smirk. He could feel electric intensity humming in the air. They stashed the money at the Indigo for the time being. One of them, the Englishman probably, had a key. They hid it there because it was close and because if Mr. Parker got wise, they could play it straight. Doyle had to think fast. Sid would return just as soon as he knew it was clear, and he'd take the money. Then he, that short fuck, and the money were gone for good. And Mr. Parker wouldn't get a dime.

Doyle walked to the door, turned around. He figured the Englishman popped the trunk; the other guy took the bag to the room. His brain thought hard and fast, processing the information.

He walked down the hall, checking doors. He came to a big closet on the left, pushed it open and saw the duffel bag which had been pitched on the carpet and knocked over a plastic mop bucket. Suddenly everything became real, and he was forced to change his plan. Doyle ran back to the other room to get his tools.

Big Tony sat behind the donut shop and did a rail of cocaine off his glass mirror that read Cowboy Roy's Fantasyland across the top. The tinted windows of the Lincoln concealed his identity well as he chopped up lines from an impressive pile of superior blow.

He snorted a broad fluffy line up the right nostril and basked in the immediate tranquility cocaine offered. A quick shot of lightning slammed his forehead, and he squeezed the wheel with both hands.

He parked next to the dumpster and watched the gray winter sky through the sunroof, listened to the wind click the frozen branches together like bones. Big Tony did a lot of coke behind that donut shop. Mr. Feeler, the owner, was into him for a little money, so when Big Tony parked behind his shop, Feeler knew better than to harass him.

In the summer he'd listen to the Little League games being played on the other side of the vine-covered fence. He'd hear the unmistakable sound of a baseball ricocheting off a bat. Birds would sing, he'd look up into the sky and watch clouds pass above him like swollen ghosts.

Somebody banged on the window hard and fast, wrenching Big Tony out of springtime. When he did, his mirror crashed to the floorboard and broke.

He drove his fist into the steering wheel when he realized it was Joey Feeler, that short, goofy fuck who managed the donut shop for his old man.

When Big Tony threw the door open, it hit Joey in the nuts and he folded like a cheap paper cup.

He dropped the white paper sack he was carrying on the pavement.

"You fuck!" Big Tony grabbed him by the throat and shoved him to the ground. He stomped Joey's head with his dress shoe, kicked him in the face. Joey interrupted his quiet time. But worse, he caused him to dump a small mountain of top shelf cocaine on the floormat. Not to mention the devastating, irrevocable trauma of breaking his favorite mirror. The one that advertised his favorite strip club.

Now it just said Cowboy Roy's Fan.

He took a step back and saw the bag full of donuts that Joey'd been generous enough to bring him lying on the ground. The bearclaw looked fresh.

Joey was rolling back and forth, howling and bleeding.

"*Awe, fuck.*" Big Tony wiped the sweat from his face with the back of his hand. He looked down at the poor bastard lying on the blacktop; he glanced over at the pastries. He thought about the cocaine. He thought about the bearclaw.

Big Tony threw a handful of cash onto the little guy's chest and told him to go clean himself up for Christ's sake. Then he scooped up the bag and eased back into the Lincoln. He left the alley with a broken mirror, half a bearclaw, and a floormat full of cocaine. And not just any run-of-the-mill cocaine, but blue-flake cocaine from Peru. *Premium Grade A Shit*, and he couldn't just let it sit there on the floormat, mixed in with the winter grit.

He was about to thrust his finger down into the pile when a patrol car rolled up behind him. Big Tony began to sweat, but he stayed in character. He had to use caution, so he kept the car where it was and played it cool.

He watched his speed, tried to think about something

else. He wasn't too worried about the Lincoln, either. It was pretty clean as far as stolen cars went. Except for the gun between the seats. And the cocaine.

Big Tony checked the right lane and hit his blinker. When he got over, he let off the gas and the cop passed. The officer gave a transitory glance in his direction and Big Tony nodded. It took a while before he could relax. He needed to take the edge off. Maybe he had enough time to hit Cowboy Roy's and see his girls. Maybe he could find a new mirror.

Joe Parker was already having a bad day, and having to run by the Indigo to pick up something his wife forgot only made things worse. He couldn't believe a piece of paper was causing him so much difficulty.

He needed the bill-of-sale for a truck he was unloading; only he'd forgotten it at home. He called his wife, Cathy, from the pay phone on the corner of 6th and Williams, the phone he always used for business, and she promised to bring it with her when she left. But then Cathy forgot it too.

He yelled into the other room, told Sid he had a job for him.

Sid entered the office eagerly; he was looking for an excuse to leave.

"What do you need, Mr. Parker?"

"You guys take care of that *situation*?" Parker liked to articulate everything in code. He didn't trust anyone, so he never came out and said anything criminal. He'd just hint around.

"Yeah, well we tried, but we had kind of a problem. Seems old No Nuts over here lost the keys."

Mr. Parker turned a burnt orange around his cheeks and

neck. Said, "Goddammit, No Nuts, you short, fat fuck. What do I even pay you for anyway?"

Johnny looked at Sid for help, but he took a step back.

"Hey boss, we didn't know. And we ain't even sure I'm the one lost 'em anyhow."

Sid turned his head to the side. "Well, you apologized for losin' 'em, Johnny, didn't you?"

"No, I wasn't sorry that I lost 'em, I was just sorry you couldn't find 'em, is all. There's a difference, trust me."

No one spoke for a second or two. Sid told No Nuts, "That doesn't even make sense."

"Just shut the fuck up!" Mr. Parker shouted. "Both uh you cocksuckers. *Who gives a fuck?* Johnny, it's your fault. It's always your fault."

Johnny stuck his wounded chest out. "Oh, it's always my fault, huh? Oh, okay. That's fine. Guess it's all my fault then."

"Everything's your fault, No Nuts," Mr. Parker said.

He thought for a few minutes, said, "Fuck 'em then. We'll just forget about this whole fucking mess. Leave the car at Montgomery's."

He looked at Sid, but paused before he spoke. "So, there's nothing to talk about?" His way of asking Sid if Telly'd been tortured for information, murdered, cut into eight individual pieces, and properly disposed of in various sections of the Mississippi, Missouri, and Meramec rivers.

"Nothing at all to talk about." Sid's way of confirming everything had been taken care of and there was no sign of the money.

"So there's nothing, *at all*, to talk about?" He wanted to make damn sure there was absolutely no chance Telly had the money.

Sid shook his head from side to side. He said it was a shame about Bruiser.

Mr. Parker dismissed his comment as if he hadn't heard, but Joe Parker's eyes were sharp chips of cobalt that missed nothing. Sid watched the lines come together under his dull brown complexion, baked and tanned from years in the sun. His hairline was failing him slightly and his chin drew together weakly, but he was as formidable an opponent as any.

"Okay then. I need you to run by my place, get somethin' off the table. You still have your key, right?"

"Of course I do." Sid patted the outside of his pocket.

"Well, run by the Indigo and grab that bill-of-sale off the table."

Sid raised his eyebrows but didn't say anything.

"It's for that Chevy half ton from South County," Parker said.

Sid nodded and rubbed the stubble on his face as if he were thinking of something brilliant to say.

"I can do that, Mr. Parker," he replied. "Should I take No Nuts here with me?" No Nuts started to object but Mr. Parker beat him to it.

"Fuck yes," he said. "Otherwise you'll rob me blind, you limey bastard."

Sid shrugged and left the office. No Nuts followed him out to the car.

"Thanks a lot, asshole," No Nuts said.

"Hey, I had to make it look good didn't I?"

"Fuck that asshole."

"Yeah, fuck that asshole is right, Johnny."

They pulled out of the parking lot and Sid turned on his heated seat. It was a bitter wintry day with dark skies and solid wind. It was a good thing he was moving to Florida tonight, No Nuts thought.

"I know we ain't had much time to talk about this, but you're sure you wanna do this, right?"

"What?" Johnny said. "Keep the money? Fuck yes I wanna keep the money. Fuck Parker. You hear how that son-of-a-bitch talked to me back there, Sid?"

"Yeah, I heard him."

Sid had an apartment in the city with a lot of nice furniture and a wardrobe straight out of Calvin Klein, but he didn't give a shit about any of that. He only needed a few things then he was free to go. Sid traveled light. No wife, no girlfriend worth remembering, just rumors of a daughter back in Manchester.

No Nuts had an ex-wife and three kids. It didn't take an IQ of 178 to know he was going to fuck everything up for himself if they kept the money. But that wasn't Sid's problem.

Sirens came up from behind them and No Nuts jumped.

"Calm down mate, it's a fire truck."

They both gave an uneasy snicker.

They pulled over to wait for the fire truck to pass, and No Nuts concentrated on the windshield wipers. Back and forth in their programmed rhythm. No Nuts asked Sid where he was going to run to.

Sid looked over, "Maybe we shouldn't tell each other." He shrugged, No Nuts nodded. Probably for the best.

Using the steering wheel controls, Sid turned the volume up suddenly when he heard something about the credit union. It was a news flash on 105.7 *The Point*. They announced the name of the man killed in the hold up, but neither Sid nor No Nuts recognized him.

"What was Bruiser's real name?"

"Hell if I know," No Nuts said. "Wasn't he Italian?"

"He thought he was."

Sid pulled back onto the road, and the big car threw mush all over the side.

No Nuts was nervous and Sid could tell.

"So where you gonna go, Johnny?"

"I thought we wasn't gonna tell?"

"Fuck it. What's it gonna hurt?"

No Nuts looked over at Sid. "I was thinkin' Florida. Ever been there?"

Sid's knuckles flashed with heat as he gripped the wheel. What were the odds of that? He couldn't let No Nuts go to Florida. *He* was going to Florida.

"Ah, you don't wanna go there, mate. *That* I can tell you."

Johnny looked puzzled.

Sid had to act quickly. "Remember Steve Bruce? Everybody called him Junior?"

No Nuts was searching. He raised his hand, tilted a little from side to side. Said, "Kind of."

"Well, Steve Jr. was about to get pinched so he hightailed it down to Panama Beach. You remember that, right?"

Johnny didn't remember. "What the fuck're you talkin' about Sid?"

"For fuck's sake, Johnny. I'm trying to tell you a story that might save your life. Now pay attention why dontchya."

No Nuts raised his shoulders and turned his palms up. "Jesus, calm down already. I hear what yer sayin'."

Sid needed to cool off. He cracked the window; it was getting tough to breathe. The Lexus was a steel crockpot and he was slow-cooking in his heated leather chair. Sid turned down the heat controls on his seat to low. He turned Johnny's up to high.

"So this guy, Steve Jr., he steals some money and gets caught. Makes a deal to save his ass, all he has to do is testify against the guy set this whole thing up."

"What thing, Sid? You lost me with this."

Sid was losing patience. "The point is, Johnny," he growled. "The point is, *fucking don't go to Florida.* They'll find you, just like they found Steve Jr. And they'll cut your dick off like they did his."

"They cut his dick off?"

Sid told him they did. Wasn't that long ago he saw something like that on the telly.

The Lexus made a right in front of the Indigo, waited for a snowplow to turn around, then they pulled into the parking garage. Sid turned the car off with the wipers in mid-wipe. Things couldn't have worked out better.

"We take the bag with us, Johnny. We'll keep it in the car until the end of the day, then we split it up and we go our separate ways. But not to Florida."

Johnny said he could live with that.

D oyle pulled package after package of cash from the duffel bag and stuffed it in the hockey bag. The bills were in stacks of $10s, $20s, $50s, and $100s. They were wrapped individually in color-coded bands. He couldn't believe no dye packs managed to find their way into the bag. Doyle knew that once a dye pack explodes, it releases an aerosol of red smoke and dye. The robbery becomes pointless, and the unlucky bastard usually tosses the bag to the ground. But this time it didn't happen, which surprised Doyle.

When the hockey bag was full of money, Doyle manhandled the oxyacetylene torch from one bag to the other; he shoved his portable hydraulic jack beside it. Along with both the sledgehammers, two hacksaws, a fifty-foot extension cord, a ballpeen hammer, a pair of asbestos gloves, a welder's helmet, a chain, and a come-along winch.

The hockey bag was just as heavy as before; he struggled to carry it back toward the front door.

He turned to take one last look at the room; he wanted to be sure he hadn't forgotten anything. Then remembered the loose cash back in the safe, plus the overpowering allure of that watch. He set the duffel bag on the floor and made a run for the safe. He decided to take what he could before he left.

Doyle returned to the living room with the jewelry, the cufflinks, the watch, and the dildo. As he stuffed the goods into his pilfer bag, he heard the unmistakable voice of that English cocksucker on the other side of the door talking to a guy he'd called No Nuts.

Johnny was already telling Sid he was hungry when they stepped from the elevator. They rounded the corner and Sid told him, "Well, we should go through his bloody fridge. I'll let you make me a sandwich while yer at it."

No Nuts laughed. "Yeah, maybe just this once."

Sid unlocked the door and they stepped into Joe Parker's living room.

He called out for Cathy Parker; just to be sure she hadn't come home for lunch.

When Sid felt confident they were alone, they turned and went down the hall.

They never saw the curtains moving as Doyle stepped out onto the balcony with the hockey bag full of cash.

The first thing they did was walk to the closet and check for the bag. They looked at each other, grinning. Sid nodded, said, "We did it, Johnny."

Johnny still couldn't believe it. He wanted to spit in Parker's face for all the abuse he'd taken over the years. He wished he could see the look on Joe Parker's face when he realized he and Sid just *restole* his stolen money.

They walked back into the kitchen and Sid opened up the fridge. He removed a jug of orange juice, took a big shot from the bottle. He opened up the crisper, removed a package of deli meat and crammed it in his mouth. "This is pretty good shit, Johnny."

Johnny didn't answer.

Sid rummaged through a few cabinets but didn't see anything worth pinching. His mind was in overdrive, his thoughts spiraling. He had to maintain his cool. Had to think things through. Once Parker realized the money was on the street he'd know the first two guys to chop up.

And it wouldn't just be Parker, but the people Parker worked for. People with connections in New Jersey and worse.

Sid finished slamming the bottle of Tropicana. He looked around, but he couldn't find No Nuts.

"Hey, Johnny?"

Johnny yelled something from the other room.

Sid walked into the bedroom, asked, "What the bloody hell. . ." But he stopped mid-sentence. Johnny No Nuts was squating on the Parker's bed with his pants rolled down to ankles, propping his back up against the headboard, pissing and shitting on Joe Parker's silk pillow.

"Good Christ, Johnny! You've bloody lost it mate, haven't you?"

Sid was drunk with laughter; he stepped back out of the bedroom in tears. No Nuts was shitting on the boss' pillow. *Son-of-a-bitch.* It looked like there was no turning back now.

D oyle had rehearsed this situation from the balcony of the room he was supposedly checking out for his parents. He *prepared* for it. Just in case he'd have to climb up onto the balcony above. Something he could do, but not with a hockey bag full of money weighing him down.

Cautiously and with great reluctance, he tossed the bag off the ledge. He watched it fall slowly then crash to the ground in an explosion of snow and ice. He'd have to come back around the building to recover it later. He just hoped nobody came across it while they were out walking their dog. The irony of stealing stolen money only to lose it to some curious resident with a schnauzer was difficult to bear.

With the pilfer bag firmly attached to his belt, Doyle grabbed the bottom of the balcony above him and pulled himself up. The dildo poked him in the stomach as he shimmied. He tried to remember why he stole it.

When he practiced the climb two months ago, it was October. The weather was 68 degrees and sunny. There were no gale force winds. Nor was there ice. And when he practiced, he never actually made the climb, but he *did* eyeball it. In his mind Doyle was pretty sure he could do it.

He held the railing tight and worked his hands up over the top until he could find the concrete ledge with his knee. Anyone driving by the Indigo and paying attention would see a man in a dark jumpsuit dangling two hundred feet up. His left hand slipped momentarily—the metal was enclosed in ice, difficult to grip—but he was finally able to pull himself up over the top and fall onto the floor of the terrace. He lay on the ground long enough to find his breath, but he had to get that money.

The one comfort he reserved was the knowledge the unit above the Parker's was vacant. A stroke of luck admittedly, and a deciding factor that allowed him to do the job in the first place.

After breaking in through the sliding door, Doyle walked across the empty apartment and through the front door of

Apartment 302, exactly one floor above Parker's apartment. He took the first elevator down. He was still nervous and sweating like a cross-country runner, despite the astringent cold.

The elevator stopped on the next floor. When the door opened, a stranger stepped inside and gave Doyle the once-over. The stranger noticed the sweating.

"Hot out there, huh sport?"

Doyle recognized the accent. It was that British asshole.

Doyle shook his head. Sweat was running down his face and raining on the floor. When he looked down, Doyle remembered his pilfer bag was still attached to his waist. He wondered if English Sid would see the outline of Mrs. Parker's dildo.

Doyle got off on the first floor. He assumed Sid was going down to the parking garage, but he wanted off that elevator the first chance he had. He cursed the fucking luck he was having. He knew the Englishman had to recognize him. Any minute now the shit would hit the fan and Doyle'd be fucked.

He walked as fast as he could down the hall, then made a right, found the exit he needed. When he opened the door, he saw the bag waiting in a quiet nook between two shrubs. Doyle grabbed the duffel bag and the expression on his face was a mix of pride, excitement, and satisfaction.

And worry. He couldn't believe it. It was too easy.

Doyle got back to the van, and his heart thumped loud enough that everyone in the garage could hear it. The scene in the elevator was too fucking close. He was sure English Sid recognized him. He had to. It was a small city.

They'd seen each other around, most recently at Cowboy Roy's not two months ago. Doyle was pretty sure Sid had been nailing one of the strippers on a semi-regular basis. He couldn't remember her name, but he was sure he could ID her by her tits. Something about her rack just left an indelible impression in Doyle's mind.

He'd have to ask Big Tony about her. Big Tony knew all the strippers at Cowboy Roy's and tracked all of their personal comings and goings for his own amusement.

Doyle'd sent him a text earlier that said: *Meet me at titled kilt in St. Charles. 1 hour*. Although he couldn't imagine Big Tony's fat fingers pawing the keyboard with legitimate success, he at least hoped he'd managed to read the message.

They needed someplace new. They couldn't trust Cowboy Roy's. They had to stay low until they could get out of town. Doyle knew the perfect place.

Doyle opened the bag and pulled out a package of $100 dollar bills. He put his nose down in the bag and smelled all the money. Split three ways, it was still a fortune worth dying for.

So far, everything they'd done was worth the risk.

He walked to the back of the van and dumped the money on the floor. He wanted to hide as much as he could before he had to divide the rest up. He deserved an extra share. He'd done all the work.

Doyle stuffed piles of cash into the toolboxes he had in the back. He stashed bundle after bundle in a roll of carpet, hid a few more stacks of hundreds under a blanket. He put the rest back into the hockey bag.

Once he assumed the Lexus was long gone, he stripped out of his jumpsuit, changed into a pair of khakis with a button-down shirt and a winter coat with a hood. He didn't look anything like the man in dark coveralls who walked around the building and picked up a hockey bag full of money. He didn't look anything like the man English Sid talked to in the elevator. At least that was what he hoped.

Doyle left the Indigo, escaped the Central West End, and made his way to Interstate 44, which he took to Interstate 270. Ten minutes later he walked into the Tilted Kilt and ordered a double cheeseburger, onion straws, and a root beer. The regulars did shots as a big guy in a Pearl Jam t-shirt destroyed the other regulars in a trivia contest.

Doyle watched the girls in their trademark low-cut uniforms with their short skirts that stopped just below each ass cheek. His waitress was Courtney; she was beautiful and he gave her a twenty-dollar tip. The hair fell around her face in dangling strands, and he fought every urge to tell her to quit her job and move away with him to their own private island, where they would spend the rest of their lives fucking and doing cartwheels on the beach.

While Sid waited for No Nuts in the Lexus, he scrolled through his phone, scouting the different locations in Florida for him to call home. He raced out of the room once he saw No Nuts depositing his stool sample on the pillow. He told No Nuts to bring the bag downstairs with him when he came.

Sid was listening to Howard Stern on satellite radio and having a good laugh when Johnny finally made it down to the car. When No Nuts stepped from the service elevator Sid could read the distraught lines that were carved deep in his worried face. He popped the trunk, but No Nuts walked up to the driver's side and dropped the duffel bag on the ground. Sid noted the bag made a weird *tink* sound when it hit concrete.

"What the fuck is this?"

"Somebody robbed us, Sid. Somebody robbed Parker.

They broke into his safe and they took our money. They filled the bag with scuba gear or somethin'."

Sid did a double take. "*Scuba gear?* What the fuck are you talkin' about, Johnny?"

No Nuts bent down and unzipped the bag to show his partner the acetylene tank and the sledgehammers. He held up a pair of asbestos gloves.

Sid looked up, his eyes as big as the pewter salad plates at Scupper Jack's. He slammed his palm against the side of his door. "*What the fuck is this?*"

"Fuck if I know. After I finished takin' a shit, I went into the bathroom to wash my hands and saw the safe open. Where the fuck is our money, Sid?"

Sid was thinking. He looked around, told No Nuts to get in the car.

"We gotta get outta here, Johnny."

He threw the bag of tools in the trunk and jumped into the passenger seat.

Sid looked around the parking garage. He tried to figure things out. At first he thought Parker'd set him up, but that didn't make any sense. He tried to think, but No Nuts kept going on about how they were fucked. How Mr. Parker'd hang their nut sacks from a pike.

"Shut the fuck up, Johnny. I gotta think. Use your bloody head for once and help me."

The clues were there in the bag. A torch, heavy-duty gloves, sledgehammers, hydraulic jacks, gauges to measure heat temperatures. Somebody planned a job, a serious job, but they didn't end up using the gear. *Why?* Because they just so happened to find a large bag filled with money in a closet.

Sid glanced down at his watch and did the math. Whoever robbed Parker did it within a two-hour window from the time No Nuts set the money in the closet and the time they got back.

Sid opened the door and got out of the car. Somebody'd been following them. That was the only thing that made sense. Sid couldn't figure it out how it all happened, but he was completely devastated by the sudden realization he had been so close to the money and now it was gone. GONE. And he had no idea who took it or how he'd ever get it back.

No Nuts opened his door and started to get out, but Sid told him to forget it. They had to call Mr. Parker and tell him he'd been robbed. His stolen money, stolen once, had just been stolen again.

They pulled out of the lot, and Sid drove to another parking lot directly across from the Indigo's parking garage. He sat embracing the quiet; he needed to think.

The only sound they heard were the wipers sliding across the windshield until finally Sid broke the silence. He told No Nuts that tweaker fuck Telly must've been smarter than they gave him credit for. The whole time he was working with another guy besides Bruiser. He must've had this silent partner following him just in case.

"Yeah, but that don't add up, Sid. If the guy had a partner why'd he leave the money in the trunk for us to find it? Then let us take it, just to go through the trouble of stealing it back. That don't make any sense."

Fuck! Sid pounded the steering wheel as the snow continued to fall, alternating between hard and light, but never letting up.

"Why'd Telly meet in the first place if he had the money?" No Nuts asked.

"Fuck if I know, Johnny. Maybe he was waitin' to get hooked up before he left town. But who the fuck knows?

Last thing I'd wanna do is try and speculate on the mindset of a fucking tweaker."

"Maybe he didn't think we'd kill him?"

"No shit, Johnny. You bloody well right he didn't think we'd kill him."

No Nuts shrugged and chewed on his thumbnail.

They knew Telly was just a pawn. He was a disposable tweaker who took the blame so the cops could close the case and there'd be swift justice for the city. Regardless of who ended up with the money, Telly ended up dead. That's how it was supposed to work. But nobody counted on Bruiser taking hot lead in the back.

The anxiety hit No Nuts harder than it hit Sid. "What're we gonna do, man? We are so fucked."

Sid knew there was professional grade burglary equipment in that bag. Somebody came to the Indigo ready to steal the whole bloody building. Whoever stole their money was prepared for anything.

"Whoever hit Parker was a pro," Sid said. "Telly was just a bloody tweaker. No way they coulda been workin' together, Johnny."

"So how the fuck does some pro find out about this shit if there's only five or six of us who knows?"

Sid shook his head and said he didn't know. He was looking through the windshield when a Chevy van that said Naramore Locksmith Co. on the side pulled out of the Indigo.

He squinted to get a better look at the driver, then looked over at No Nuts.

"You see that van, Johnny?"

"Yeah, the locksmith guy? What about it? Think we just got robbed by a locksmith?"

Sid checked his rear-view mirror and slapped the shifter

into reverse. "I dunno, Johnny, but I got a funny feelin'. Maybe it's nothin', but let's look into it."

Sid thought about that elevator ride. There was somethin' about that guy in the coveralls. Sid knew him but he couldn't remember from where. Just something about him—thieves' intuition.

Sid slid out of the parking lot with his iPhone in his right hand, searching with his thumb. "What'd that van say, Johnny? Naramore Locksmith Company?"

"Yeah, somethin' like that." No Nuts turned around to make sure there was no traffic coming up behind them while Sid was on his phone. "Clear," he said. Sid got over.

"Well, well, what do you make of this? There's no bloody Naramore Locksmith I can find." He turned the screen toward No Nuts.

"What's this mean, Sid?"

"I'm not sure what it means yet, but I think I might've just seen this cocksucker in the elevator."

"This guy in the van?"

"Maybe. Whoever I saw was sweatin' his arse off. He looked nervous." Sid remembered the bulging fanny pack around Doyle's waist, could've been anything in there.

"Sid, the light!"

Sid was lost in thought. He blazed through a red light and got hit hard in the back passenger side by a ¾ ton GMC. It spun the car around four times. Sid slammed into a few trashcans and sent them crashing out into the street. The front of the Lexus knocked down a wooden privacy fence, and one of the boards broke free and shattered the windshield.

"Bloody fuck!" Sid said. Everything happened fast. He looked down to find the car still running. He put it in reverse and it made a horrible sound, but it went. Sid cut the wheel hard to the left, shoved it up into drive, and hammered the accelerator, throwing snow all over the young couple who stopped to help. No one climbed out of the GMC, the front windshield spiderwebbed.

No Nuts moved slowly. He'd been out cold for a minute, maybe two. Sid asked him if he was all right.

"My head's killin' me, Sid."

Sid took a look at him. "You'll be fine, Johnny."

The Lexus was fucked, but Sid didn't care anymore. All he cared about was the stolen money and the cocksucker who'd re-stolen it from them. As hard as he tried, he could only make a single connection. The credit union manager, the one Bruiser and Telly took care of.

"My fuckin' head's killin' me, Sid."

"Toughen up, Johnny. Would ya look at my bloody Lexus fer fuck's sake?"

No Nuts rubbed the knot on the side of his head and told Sid fuck his Lexus.

"What should we do about Parker, Johnny? We call him, tell him he's been robbed, or let him find out on his own? We could just tell him we grabbed the paper off the table and we don't say shit about the robbery. He ain't gonna know when he got hit anyway."

No Nuts said that was a great idea.

"Fuck it, we're not tellin' him then. Far as we know, if he asks us we don't know what he's talking about."

Sid lost track of the van, and the Lexus was making unhealthy noises. He pulled over into the parking lot of a grocery store to call Parker. He'd tell him they had the paper, but there'd been a slight fender-bender. They'd be there soon as they could.

"What about that locksmith?"

Sid smiled devilishly, said he shouldn't be too hard to find.

He was pretty sure he'd seen him around over at Cowboy Roy's Fantasyland.

Big Tony sat in his favorite booth at Cowboy Roy's and sipped expensive cognac and dreamed about a woman he could never have. She moved slowly, with purpose. More in love with herself than she could ever love anyone else. But that was okay with him. He wanted to watch her dance. Watch her body speak to him as he sipped Remy Martin. The good shit.

When she finished touching herself and grinding on the pole, the crowd of losers gathered around her pulled crumpled dollar bills from their shallow pockets and tossed them down on the stage. Big Tony thought that was unacceptable.

He walked up to the stage like a hot shot and threw her a handful of stiff twenties. It was a bold move, but he was now a high roller. He was about to make an extravagant score; he was feeling flush. He'd lure her in, ensnare her with the Jacksons, and get her out to the Lincoln. He'd break out the Peruvian nasal therapy and he was guaranteed a blowjob. Or at least a quick tug.

He took his seat and waited for her to come and thank him, but she snatched the money off the stage and disappeared behind the curtains. The brief fantasy that flashed through his head suddenly flamed up and disappeared into ashes. Not to mention the sixty bucks.

He slammed the rest of his Remy and dropped the empty glass on the table. *Fuck it.* The clock was winding down. It was almost time to roll, but he left Cowboy Roy's one pissed off son-of-a-bitch and vowed never to return. He should've known better than to go on a Wednesday afternoon.

My phone rang and woke me from a power nap. It was Big Tony. He said there was a lot going on and we should talk. I told him I could meet him at the club in an hour, but he said that was a no-go. We had to meet someplace different. He gave me the address. Said he had to go, better keep the line clear. He thought Doyle might've just tried to call him.

I walked into the bathroom and splashed water on my face. I looked at my reflection in the mirror and flexed. My abdominals were getting soft, but they still hardened on command. My shoulders were round and hard enough.

I looked back across the room at my heavy bag and my weight bench. It sat with two 45's on each side, all of it collecting dust. When I turned to the side and flexed my triceps, I was impressed to still see the outline of a nice horseshoe shape in the muscle, considering my failure to work out with any regularity.

"What do you think, Frank?" I struck a front double bicep pose, but he didn't look impressed.

"Hungry, pal?" Frank dropped low and barked. I walked over to my desk, and he went crazy when I pulled open the food drawer. He danced and jumped and peeled out.

I dumped the very last beer can full of dog food on the floor. I'd need to restock while I was out. I couldn't find his water bowl and could see it wasn't in the usual corner where he liked to drag it. The water from the bathroom faucet was starting to smell funny anyway, so I dumped half a Corona in the coffee pot I no longer used, then I left for the meeting with my associates.

On my way to the Tilted Kilt, I had a glass of vodka

mixed with cranberry juice and a dash of peach schnapps. The snow continued to fall; I saw a handful of cars nestled in the ditches by the time I made it to the interstate. I wanted to find out what Doyle and Big Tony'd dug up. I'd spent my whole day with Amish Ron waiting for him to let his guard down long enough so I could steal something. I realized Detective Ron Beachy wasn't the type of guy to make mistakes. He wasn't going to tell me anything I didn't need to know. He didn't trust me.

I sucked a mouthful of liquid strength up my straw and changed lanes. I smashed the pedal to the floor for a second and let that Crown Victoria speak to me. I'd pounded a handful of So Co's back at my place, and I was now working the bottom end of my second Styrofoam cup, driving the orange plastic straw into the little crevices to locate every last drop of Stoli.

As I greeted the initial feelings of intoxication with open arms, I began to notice my thoughts becoming more lucid with every drink I mixed. Like a lighting bolt from above, I realized the core truth of my life—drinking more made me a better detective.

I was putting things together and filling in the blanks. One day, the world would marvel at my detective genius. And although the legacy I would leave behind would be littered with empty beer cans, at least I was leaving a trail of some kind to be discovered.

After exhausting the contents of the cup, I set it where it fit tight between the seats and the 12-gauge. I slipped the lid off, poured a little Stoli on whatever ice cubes were left, and I did a good job of holding the Vic on the road considering the circumstances. Only an experienced drunk could mix a drink with one hand while navigating his way through a snowstorm at high speeds with the other.

When I slid the Vic sideways into the parking lot, I saw Big Tony's Lincoln parked in the far corner with him still behind the wheel. Probably doing cocaine. I took a powerful swig from the cup and parked beside him. He motioned for me to get in.

"It's fucking cold outside." I sat down.

Big Tony looked at me. "Ain't that the truth?"

He had the mirror resting on his leg, and I saw it was broken. I watched him stare off into space; he was still holding the straw between his thumb and his finger.

I pointed to the mirror, but he shook his head. Said, "Don't ask."

He played with the straw in his hand.

"Y'know," I said, "it's better to use a bill."

"Huh?" Big Tony squinted at me.

"It's better to use a bill to do lines. If a cop pulls you over, there's just a bill. Maybe it's got residue on it, maybe it doesn't. But either way, you're gonna say you just got it from the clerk at the last gas station you stopped at. You can always blame somebody else. If you get pulled over with a straw in your pocket that's only two inches long. . ."

"They're gonna think you was doin' coke."

"Well, I'll go out on a limb here and say it'll raise their level of suspicion."

I took another drink from my cup and hoped he would spare me a return lecture about driving drunk in a snowstorm. At this stage in my career I was much better suited to give advice than to receive it.

"Here's Doyle."

We watched him walk across the parking lot, rubbing his hands in front of him. Doyle dove into the backseat and ordered Big Tony to turn the fucking heat up quick.

"It's already on high."

Doyle looked around. "This piece of shit doesn't have rear heat?"

"Watch it you cocksucker." Big Tony took a great deal of pride in his stolen Town Car.

"Maybe you'll just have to buy a new one with your cut."

I looked back at Doyle, beaming.

Big Tony was too big to turn around so he burned holes in Doyle's forehead through the rear-view as he looked down and pulled something from his pants pocket.

"What the fuck're you talkin' about?"

"I'm talkin' about this, man." Doyle tossed a bundle of $100 bills into the front seat.

I almost spilled my drink. "Doyle, what the fuck?"

He pitched another stack of Franklins up front. I couldn't believe it. Finally, something good was happening.

The next few minutes were filled without words or complete sentences. Just three now-rich guys, one of us coked up, one of us half-drunk, but all yelling and laughing, slapping each other's shoulders and backs.

Doyle said he hadn't had time to count it, but each stack of hundreds held fifty bills. "So that's like five thousand dollars you're holding," he said, doing the math.

"So how many stacks of five thousand are there?" Big Tony asked.

"Maybe a hundred. Maybe two hundred. I don't know exactly."

Stunned, Big Tony and I looked at each other with open mouths. No one could stop smiling.

"We could be lookin' at a million dollars?" I asked.

Doyle said maybe.

I finished off the rest of my vodka and gripped the cash tightly in my hand. My first question was how much Doyle put back for himself but I didn't ask. He did all the work and I knew I would've done the same thing. If I could walk away from this with a few hundred grand who was I to complain?

"I'm going to Florida," Doyle said.

Big Tony slipped a fat Don Pepin Garcia between his lips and said he was going to Vegas.

Now that we actually had the money, I didn't know what to do with it. I couldn't move too fast; it would look suspicious. I couldn't spend the money in the same city it was taken from with any degree of comfort. Not to mention that Amish Ron's bullshit detector was on high alert. Sooner or later I'd end up as a suspect. Maybe that's why the Chief had the Amishman watching me so close. The thought suddenly occurred to me I didn't have a place to store that much loot. I couldn't start filling my sad, overdrawn bank account with cash stolen from a credit union.

I shook the ice in my cup and announced I was ready for a drink, but Doyle told me to hang on a minute. He may have bad news.

That was the moment I started wishing I hadn't gotten involved. The moment he said we'd have trouble. I knew there was no such thing as a free ride. Everything came with a price. Especially a duffel bag full of money other men died for.

"What do you mean, you *may* have some bad news?"

Doyle put his head down, shook it from side to side and said, "Well, I guess you could say I *do* have some bad news. That English bastard got in the elevator with me on the way down. I'm pretty sure he recognized me."

"What?" Big Tony demanded.

"*You're pretty sure he recognized you?*" I screeched.

Doyle said it was true. He felt bad about it.

"*Jesus Christ,* we're fucked now," Big Tony said.

116

"We're gonna end up in a Federal Prison gettin' our assholes stretched out by convicts," I said.

Doyle waved his hands. "Hang on a minute. There must be something we can do."

"Like what, run? Cuz that's about all we can do."

"No, that ain't all we can do," Doyle said.

I knew where this discussion was headed. The only place it could go.

"What do you suggest?" Big Tony asked. "We kill 'em?"

"It's something to consider."

I told them it wouldn't be a bad idea, but I knew we couldn't just start killing people. Enough people'd died already. Besides, I knew Amish Ron was all over this case, and he wasn't giving up.

Big Tony said, "Valentine, use some of your police connections and see what you can dig up."

I said I would, told them I'd already started poking around.

"The problem's Ron Beachy. He's a detective and a real ballbuster. The kinda guy who lives to do the right thing. Kinda guy who tells his boss when he's been overpaid."

"What kind of asshole are we dealing with?" Big Tony demanded.

"The kind of asshole that spent his whole life churning butter. And now there's a chip on his shoulder the size of Rhode Island." Big Tony raised an eyebrow in confusion, so I tried to explain. I told him Ron was raised Amish. He did everything the hard way. But now he was a cop, and he was damn good at what he did.

I told them he didn't have any unsolved cases, just cases he hadn't solved yet.

Big Tony busted out a mighty hoot. "You're bullshitting me, Valentine. You gonna tell me he pulls people over in a buggy?"

Now Doyle laughed. "Wouldn't a siren scare the horses, Nick?"

"I don't think you fuckers understand. He's good, this guy. Best I ever seen."

Big Tony asked if Ron had a beard.

I was playing on both teams and I had to make a decision quick before I got called out.

Doyle said, "Well, I dunno about you guys, but I'm gettin' the fuck outta here while I can. It's still early. Nobody knows nothin' about nothin'. There ain't never gonna be a better time to run than now."

Big Tony couldn't decide one way or the other, and I couldn't blame Doyle for leaving. It was the only move he could make in his position. I figured that Big Tony should probably run too.

I was the only one who couldn't leave. There were too many questions, and I was right in the middle of everything. Part of me wanted to help the Chief. Part of me wanted to help Amish Ron. But most of me wanted that money if I didn't have to kill anyone to get it.

I told Doyle, "You gotta do what you gotta do. Runnin' may be your best chance."

Doyle told us Parker's guys were pretty hardcore. It looked like they'd killed the tweaker.

He showed me a license plate number to the car parked at Montgomery's. Said it must be the tweaker's ride, but they'd been damn surprised to find the money by the looks of it.

"*Surprised?*" I asked.

"It looked like they was about to leave, then that short dumb fuck gets out and checks the trunk. He's so stunned to find the money he falls on his ass and slides halfway under the car."

I grabbed the piece of paper and crammed it in my

pocket. It sounded like Parker's boys were going to keep the money for themselves, but then Doyle came along and fucked that up.

"This is good news," I said. "Parker doesn't even know he's been robbed." I laughed. "We're clean, far as Parker goes. Parker doesn't know he ever *had* the money. And those two fucks, they can't even say anything to him or he'll know they took it first." I elbowed Big Tony's arm, saw him nodding. "Parker will never even know he was robbed."

Big Tony burst out laughing. He tapped on that box which held the coke. He said it was really great news.

I noticed Doyle wasn't saying much.

I asked him if there anything else we should know.

Doyle said there was.

"I took some, uh, loose change. Maybe a watch."

"*Goddammit Doyle!* What is it with you and those fucking watches? You could buy a hundred watches with that money." But he didn't have an answer. Pilfering was in his blood. He couldn't turn down a watch any easier than I could turn down a drink.

"Oh, you really fucked us, Doyle." Big Tony said.

Doyle said he knew it.

When they pulled into the lot at Cowboy Roy's Fantasyland, the light was fading and the corner streetlights were sputtering to life.

Sid had called Mr. Parker to tell him he was tied up with the accident. Told him he'd get him that piece of paper just as soon as he could, but said he may have to run No Nuts to the hospital first. Parker cursed Sid's incompetence and crappy driving, told him to bring that bill of sale tomorrow.

Sid told No Nuts they had to wrap this whole deal up tonight. "We don't have much time."

They searched the parking lot before they walked in but found no van. When they walked through the door, they showed the bouncer their IDs then ordered drinks. Sid recognized a few people, but he just sat with his back against the bar and let his eyes drift across the smoke-filled room.

He'd had a falling out with one of Cowboy Roy's girls a few weeks ago and hadn't been back since. He hoped he didn't see her. That was drama he didn't need.

Johnny ordered a beer, then handed one to Sid.

"What's this guy look like again?"

"Kind of average, Johnny. A little taller than you, kinda fat." Sid looked No Nuts up and down. "Bloody hell, he kinda looks like you now that I think about it."

No Nuts dropped down onto the barstool. His stomach was a mess. One minute he thought he was a millionaire, the next minute he realized he wasn't. And then he was in a fucking car wreck.

"Listen, it's gonna be okay," Sid assured him. "Johnny, we're gonna find this wanker, I swear it. I've been in here plenty. He sits right over there with some other fat fuck." Sid turned to look at Johnny. "If these cocksuckers took our money we'll know soon enough."

The longer Sid watched the crowd, the more he remembered about the place. A guy like him didn't miss much. He knew about Big Tony. Knew he'd done time; he probably knew a connected guy or two. Sid wasn't sure about his level of involvement, but he knew he was a hardcore thief. That meant his mate from the elevator was a thief too.

That meant there was a great chance they had the money.

The doorman walked by, and Sid stopped him. Said he was looking for a few of his chums and had he seen 'em?

Sid pointed to the table, said, "They usually sit right over there."

The bouncer shrugged. Told Sid, "I dunno. People come and go."

Sid leaned forward, told the door man, "I'm pretty sure one of 'ems a regular."

"Listen pal, I dunno what to tell ya. You gotta picture of this guy? What's he look like?"

"He's a fat guy. Both of 'em are actually." Sid held up two fingers.

"One of them looks like him." He pointed at No Nuts.

The bouncer said, "Look around, this place is full of fat guys." Then he walked into the back room.

"What a fucking asshole," Sid complained.

"Well, he's right." No Nuts looked at his watch.

"The night's still young, Johnny. We got plenty of time."

"Yeah Sid, I'm just a little worried. Parker ain't called yet."

Sid said No Nuts should relax.

"I wouldn't worry about it. Hell, he probably just doesn't know about it yet."

No Nuts told Sid surely a man would know something was wrong when he found a turd on his pillow. No Nuts felt that he, himself, would instinctively know such a thing.

A guy in a shirt that was much too tight leaned back on his stool and waved Sid forward. "One of those so-called buddies uh yours did this." He pointed to his damaged face. His left cheek was black, swelled to the absolute maximum; the skin around his eye was stretched tight and misshapen. It looked like any minute it could blow, covering anyone in a three-foot radius with puss.

No Nuts took a good look at his undamaged mustache. No Nuts was drawn to it, captivated by the manly power it held.

Sid took a step forward, leaned into the guy.

"What're you sayin' pal? Who tuned you up?"

"His name's Valentine. I asked around last night."

"He fat?" Sid asked. "Looks kinda like him?" Sid gestured to No Nuts.

Captain Mustache shook his head. "No, this was a good lookin' guy. Solid, with a whole lotta muscle. Bastard took a cheap shot." It looked to Sid like he'd taken several cheap shots.

Sid and Johnny looked at each other. Didn't sound like their guy.

"You said he had friends?"

He stood, turned around, and the cheap lighting illuminated the knotted bulge of flesh on the side of his face. It looked like someone had sliced his cheek open and inserted a tennis ball under the skin. He pointed across the bar, his detached retina floating madly.

"There was three of 'em right over there. The other two guys were maybe who you're lookin' for."

Sid thanked him and told the hoochie behind the bar to give the guy with the mustache a bottle of something nice. He tossed a ten-spot on the counter and told No Nuts to c'mon and they walked to the door.

Outside the wind assaulted them with cold, vicious blasts. As he started the Lexus, Sid complained again about the damage. He turned the seats on high and looked over at No Nuts.

"I know this Valentine. He's a tough guy all right. I've heard about him. Used to be a cop but he was a drunk. Always smacking people up." He made a hand gesture to No Nuts, alluding to the guy in the bar.

"That guy with that big goddamn mustache?" Johnny asked. "Valentine did that?"

Sid nodded. "Yeah. If Valentine's involved, he ain't goin' ta go easy, Johnny."

"So, we kill the motherfucker. We kill all these mother-fuckers, Sid. Because I want my goddamned money." No Nuts was breathing heavy.

Sid could see him coming unglued. "Well, it bloody well may come to that."

The Lexus was making noises Sid didn't think were possible, and they got louder as the car picked up speed.

"This thing sounds like shit," Johnny told him.

"Well you shoulda told me about that truck a little bit sooner, No Nuts."

"That's right, I forgot. Everything's always my fault."

"Awe, quitchyer bloody cryin', Johnny. If we ain't got that money by tomorrow there's gonna be at least three dead bodies to show whoever does have the money we ain't fuckin' around."

No Nuts nodded in agreement as Sid's phone rang.

"It's him, Johnny."

"Valentine?"

"Fuck no. It's Parker."

He shrugged, then answered, "Hey boss."

"Sid, where the fuck you been?"

Sid started to answer, but Parker didn't give him time.

"I need you guys back here soon as you can."

"Sure boss, no problem." Sid clicked off and locked his phone.

He told No Nuts that Parker wanted to see them both, now. He sounded pissed off.

"He must've found that open safe," No Nuts said. He was a basket case, couldn't take the stress. "*He knows, Sid!*"

"He knows dick, Johnny."

"No, he knows man. Trust me, I know he knows."

Sid took his right hand off the wheel and slapped Johnny's chest, took hold of his shirt.

"Listen ya crazy bugger, he don't know nothin'. It's just your mind fuckin' with ya, Johnny." Sid tapped his finger to his head. "It's all in your head."

No Nuts put his window down, told Sid he was going to puke.

Sid hit the brakes hard enough that No Nuts slid forward in his seat. "Not in my bloody car, Johnny."

No Nuts puked into the wind before Sid could stop the car, and blowback from the Mexican buffet coated the passenger's seat.

"No!" Sid watched it unfold in slow motion. He did all he could do; he worked the brake and pushed No Nuts closer to the window.

"You son-of-a-bitch." Sid screamed. No Nuts never said he was sorry.

We divided the cash in a hurry, the three of us crammed in the back of Doyle's van. I sat on a roll of carpet with my back against a stack of magnetic signs. Doyle would attach them to the side of his van depending on the job. Doyle was attempting to divide the money as evenly as he could when Big Tony's cell rang.

"Yeah?" he answered. He listened for a few moments, staring straight ahead, then said, "*What?*" He sat up and pulled out the cigar. "When'd this happen?"

Doyle and I were frozen.

Big Tony looked at me and I looked at Doyle, but he was

fiddling with his watch. "This guy, he British?" Big Tony asked. "His partner fat?"

Big Tony nodded his head slowly then leaned up and poked his head out the front window to see if we were being watched. I glanced behind me. The back windows were heavily tinted. It was dark, there wasn't much to see, but I still looked around.

Big Tony closed his phone and slipped it in his pocket, looked up. "Well, it's started."

Doyle continued stuffing money in the bags. I felt my cheeks burning white hot with nervous agitation.

"That was Flames, from the club," he began. "Said those cocksuckers came around lookin' for you and me." Doyle stopped for a second, more like a pause, then went back to filling trashbags with individual packages of stolen cash and muttering numbers to himself.

I needed a drink pretty bad, but I wasn't climbing out of the van until business was resolved. My .45 was at the office, but I still had the shotgun in the Vic. Not to mention the chainsaw.

"So whaddaya think we do?" Doyle asked.

I told them, "You guys need to make plans, and quick. I'd leave now. Don't go home, just drive."

Big Tony gave me a look that told me he wasn't done giving bad news.

"They're lookin' for you too, Valentine."

"Oh yeah? Your bouncer pal tell you that?" I didn't like the sound of this. There was no possible way they could know my name. "Did that cocksucker with the flames tattoos rat me out?"

"No, that cocksucker with the thirty-pound mustache did."

"Wha?" But then it hit me. That prick with the king-sized soup strainer, the one that got in my face.

"Guess he didn't like being sucker-punched," Big Tony reminded me.

I told Big Tony I took offense to such a remark and assured him I'd done nothing of the sort. I fought with lightning reflexes, using a classic battlefield strategy. There was nothing wrong with that.

"Well, now they know your name. Looks like they know all our names."

Doyle seemed oblivious to everything around him. The three of us were on a roller coaster of emotions, but Doyle performed well under the pressure.

I said, "Looks like our options are simple: Leave town or find English Sid and his partner and kill 'em. Or we wait for them to find us and do the same."

"I'll be gone by morning light," Doyle said. He looked up for the first time and smiled. "I been waitin' for a haul like this my whole life, guys. I ain't gonna fuck it up by stickin' around here and gettin' shot."

"I'm with Doyle," Big Tony said. "Let's get the fuck outta here."

They both looked at me and I told them I was right behind them, although I doubted it was true. I couldn't leave town, I had to see this through. Not for myself so much, but for the Chief. He was close to my father; he'd always looked out for me. Especially after the old man died.

Chief Caraway and his wife were the family I never had. I spent many Christmases with them. They came to my high-school graduation; the Chief bought me my first suit. They saw qualities in me that I never saw in myself.

Doyle handed me a trashbag full of money. It was heavy, but he told me not to worry. Said he'd double-bagged it just in case.

I looked them both in the eye and shook their hands. Told

them to watch their backs and have good lives. I wished them the best of luck as I climbed from the side door and hoped I wasn't stepping into a shotgun blast.

Big Tony closed the door behind me. I walked over the to Vic and dropped my Hefty bag in the trunk. The snow let up to nothing more than loose flakes drifting across the parking lot to wherever the wind took them.

I sat down behind the wheel and started the engine. I listened to the Police Interceptor fire up, then wrapped my right hand around that bottle of *Stoli,* pulled it close to me. I glanced down at the 12-gauge pump; loaded, racked, and ready to decimate any bastard unfortunate enough to stand in front of it.

I tipped the end of the bottle into my cup; poured a slow eight count. Wind slammed the car in powerful gusts as the wipers drug across the hard clumps of ice that had accumulated in the short time it took me to get a trashbag full of money and a death sentence.

I still wasn't sure who knew what, but the one thing I did know for sure was there was no turning back. I was committed. And the weight of the world bore down on me like a ten-ton sledgehammer wrapped in razor wire.

Vodka flowed into my mouth with a hint of watered-down cranberry as I put the Vic in gear. I left the Tilted Kilt with a fresh drink and roughly three hundred thousand dollars in the trunk of my car. I listened to Christmas music on the radio while I sipped on a cocktail and tried to calm my nerves.

The light turned yellow. I pushed the brake pedal slowly to bring the Vic to a gentle stop beside a salt truck. As I brought the cup to my lips, I saw a car in the rear-view mirror. There were two guys watching me.

I scanned both lanes and punched the accelerator hard enough to break traction but soft enough not to spin the tires any harder than I had to. I charged through the red light, took the first right onto Interstate 270, and did the best I could to get lost in traffic. I watched my speed and was careful not to spill my drink.

When I was convinced they were no longer behind me, I replayed everything again in my mind. It didn't look the same as it did the first time. I couldn't tell what was real anymore. Everything was mixed with the blurred perception of a drunken and chemically induced reality.

One thing was certain; it felt good to have a shotgun by my side.

My road was ahead. As far as I knew there was no one behind me. Maybe there never had been.

I took the exit, took the long way home. I finished my drink and pulled into the parking lot of a guitar shop called Hornor's. I parked the Vic next to a snowdrift and killed the headlights. My fingers tap-danced on the stock of the shotgun while I waited to be sure I wasn't followed. I didn't want any surprises when I got back to the office. I didn't want a car to roll up behind me while I was hauling a trashbag full of stolen money out of the trunk with a short barrel 12-gauge in my hand.

Satisfied I was overreacting, I pulled back out onto Blackmore road and made the short drive back to the office. I remembered I was out of dog food. Goddammit, Frank. If it wasn't one thing it was another.

I drove by the office and noticed there was a light on, but I couldn't remember if I'd done it myself. In a bad part of the city you always want it to look like you're home, even when you're not.

I wasn't taking any chances.

I pulled into the alley and let the car run with the heat on. I took a straight shot of Stoli, popped the trunk, grabbed the shotgun, and dropped the bottle onto the seat. Then I grabbed the trashbag with three hundred K and walked to the bottom of the stairs with my eyes roaming the dimly lit alley for trouble. The only sound was the background noise of a big city buried under a foot of snow and ice.

I climbed the stairs one foot at a time, my palm embracing the pistol grip as my finger bonded with the trigger. I could throw the barrel up and blast someone to Hell if they were waiting at the top of the stairs. But when I finally got there nothing waited but the stale smell of my old building welcoming me home.

I stuck my key in the door and pushed it open with my foot. Frank was dancing and snorting and running around the office like usual. He jumped onto the couch, then back to the floor. Racing to my desk, running circles around boxes I'd stacked haphazardly.

I dropped the bag onto the floor and looked around the room. It looked just as I remembered leaving it. Nothing had changed.

Frank was jumping up and down on my foot, bouncing, and barking. To my left I saw an old copy of *People Magazine* with David Hasselhoff on the cover. At some point Frank decided to lay a turd across "The Hoff's" bare chest.

"Nice work," I told Frank, and then I made for my desk, where I pulled a bottle of Strawberry Hill from the mini. I took a seat in my chair and set the shotgun on the desk. When I opened my drawer to grab the .45, Frank came running. He thought it was time for food.

I apologized, then I grabbed a few leftover Whitey's from the mini and tossed them on the floor. Frank snorted, barked, sneezed, and peeled out. He grabbed the first one in his teeth and dragged it around my desk to his usual spot.

I opened up a Corona to chase down the wine.

I looked at the trashbag and then back to both guns on the desk. Then I checked the door. I realized I would probably continue that pattern of cautionary behavior until English Sid and all his friends were dead. I leaned back in my chair and took a long, smooth gulp of wine. I swished it around in my mouth, savoring its cheap price and high alcohol content.

Frank ran back around my desk and sprang up onto my lap, landing on my nuts as usual. I sat up hard and cussed him good for his lack of consideration; he jumped up and licked my face and mouth. I pushed him off my lap and he hit the floor, but he sprang right back undeterred. I rubbed his head and told him that I liked his style. I returned a half-empty bottle of wine to the fridge, grabbed both guns, then walked to the couch and went down cold for the next ten hours.

They arrived at the Indigo in the damaged Lexus that could be heard from a mile away. Sid made No Nuts ride all the way there with his window down to help vent the putrid smell.

He told Johnny again to be cool. If Parker wanted them dead he sure as hell wouldn't be calling them to his place to do it. Johnny finally relaxed. He knew Sid was right, but he still felt like shit and smelled like puke.

When they knocked on the door they were edgy and tense, but Parker opened it immediately and set them at ease. He was wearing sweatpants. His face was bulbous and scarlet. Sid couldn't tell if he'd been drinking hard or crying hard.

Once they were inside he looked them both in the eyes and told them why he'd called them out so late.

"I got hit tonight." His face showed no reaction, but Sid could tell Parker was struggling. Parker's jaw muscle flexed on the side of his face like a clam hitting coals.

"*Hit?*" Sid did a good job of acting stunned.

Parker nodded, then walked over to the bar. He poured himself a glass of bourbon, poured another for each of his guys.

"Some motherfucker busted into my safe. Stole all the cash, some jewelry. Sick bastard even took one of Cathy's dildos." No Nuts giggled under his breath.

Parker was staring off into space. They'd never seen him this defenseless and susceptible. Parker was as distant as he'd ever been, and he struggled to maintain even a nominal focus. He took a drink and swallowed hard, then said, "The motherfucker even took a shit on my pillow." There was no way to hide the encroachment he'd suffered.

"They took a shit on your bloody pillow, boss?" Sid deserved an Academy Award for his performance, but Johnny was failing on every level. Parker swayed, said, "I think somebody wiped his asshole on my pillowcase, boys." He nodded, seemed to agree with himself, then set his glass down on the bar. He looked up at No Nuts, his complexion white and pasty. All blood appeared to have drained from No Nuts' body.

Parker thought he saw a bean on Johnny's shoulder. He finally got a good look at him and his expression shifted to drill sergeant. "My God, Johnny. You smell worse than a suitcase full of unicorn shit." He stepped closer, offered an inspection. "Good Christ, is that vomit on your shirt?" The old Parker was suddenly back, belittling No Nuts, but with good reason.

Parker looked at Sid. "What the fuck is wrong with this guy?"

Sid shrugged. "Food poisoning from a vengeful Mexican buffet."

No Nuts stood in silence.

Parker told No Nuts to go down the hall and splash cold water in his face. Have a smoke. Do something to make himself feel better. Said to trust him, he'd feel like a new man.

No Nuts said *okay*. He walked down the hall and passed the closet that once held a fortune that almost belonged to him. He found the bathroom, stuck his face down toward the faucet. He splashed handful after handful of cold water in his eyes. He stood, looked in the mirror as water ran off his nose and dripped onto the counter. He thought of how he might look with one of those cowboy mustaches.

He walked back to the living room as Parker poured another round. Sid asked Johnny if he was all right. Johnny said he was fine.

"Cathy left me for another man," Parker blurted out unexpectedly. He looked at his guys for support. "Guess I shoulda seen it coming." Sid and No Nuts looked at each other, but didn't know what to say.

"We'd been getting along fine, I thought." Parker stared off absently.

Sid finished his glass, helped himself to another. He pulled Parker's glass from his hand so he could refill it.

"Sorry to hear 'bout you and the missus," Sid offered.

"Yeah, sorry boss," No Nuts trailed.

"When I accused her of fucking around, she stormed out. Said maybe she was and maybe she wasn't."

Sid handed the boss his drink. Parker looked up, thanked him.

Sid looked at Johnny and shrugged.

"I guess you didn't call the cops, eh?" Sid asked.

Mr. Parker told Sid *fuck no* he didn't call the cops.

"Called you instead. I want you to find this cocksucker and chop his head off."

Sid was astonished. Parker never made direct threats; he was always paranoid about being recorded.

No Nuts piped up, "So you're sayin' y'know who done it boss?"

"Goddamn right I do."

There came a second where No Nuts felt like his life expectancy was heavily dependent on Parker's next sentence. He turned around to be sure some other sneaky fuck wasn't coming up behind him with a piano wire.

"It's this security guard, this cocksucker from the credit union." Parker frowned once he realized he'd actually said the words, revealing more than he'd intended. Now he was committed to finishing the story, telling his two trusted employees more than he'd ever wanted them to know.

"The credit union?" Sid asked, genuinely surprised for the first time since they'd got there.

Mr. Parker nodded, finished the drink in a long gulp. This time No Nuts grabbed his glass and refilled it. They needed to get the boss drunk.

"He was the inside guy," Parker went on. "He gave us the layout. Told us about the dye packs, about that banker, the one Bruiser and that junkie whacked. Had to get rid of that fuck so he couldn't set the dye packs out. We knew we had a window to get clean money without the chance of a dye pack, long as he didn't show up for work."

No Nuts handed him his drink. He took it, raised the glass to his lips, and said, "How'd everything get so fucked up?"

Sid liked the way the conversation was going. The more Parker talked, the stronger he felt their chances were of surviving.

"If it was all part of the plan, why'd the security guard shoot Bruiser in the back?" Sid asked.

"Fuck if I know." Parker yelled. "I been tryin' to figure this shit out for two days."

"So, how you know it's this security guard that robbed you?"

Parker slammed his glass down, liquor splashed out on the bar.

"Well, isn't it obvious? She's fucking him. That whore. I give her everything and she wants to leave me for some Rent-A-Cop cocksucker. Gives him the key to my house, the combination to my safe. Let's him take what he wants, then he *shits on my fucking pillow!*" Parker picked his glass up and flung it across the room where it shattered against the wall.

Sid realized this was their opportunity to make things right. Let Parker think it was the security guard robbed him and shit on his bed.

"Here, have a seat boss." Sid set him down on the couch. "You need to calm down, Joe. Johnny, and me, we're here for ya. We're family." Mr. Parker looked up into Sid's face, his bottom lip slightly bulged out. He thanked him with a hand to the shoulder. Said, "I really appreciate this, boys."

Sid and Johnny said no problem, it was the least they could do. Then Mr. Parker instructed No Nuts to go clean that pile of shit off his mattress and throw the sheets in the fucking trashcan.

No Nuts had started for a refill, but Parker's words stopped him cold in his tracks.

Sid was quick to meet his eyes; he told No Nuts not to fuck this up with the severe look on his face.

With great reluctance, No Nuts went to Mr. Parker's bedroom and rolled the sheets up in a ball. He searched through a few drawers and sniffed a pair of Cathy's panties from the hamper.

When he came back to the room, Parker was passed out on the couch and Sid was drinking by himself. He told No Nuts they had to go and see the security guard.

"Now?"

Sid said *yes*.

When Sid opened the door to his Lexus he gagged at the rancid smell of secondhand chalupas on his beautiful leather. He left No Nuts standing outside in the cold while he bathed the seat in expensive cologne. When No Nuts got in, he said the car smelled like Kenneth Cole and vomit.

"I don't wanna hear it, No Nuts."

They pulled out of the parking garage in the beat up Lexus and took their time getting to South County.

"Parker gave me the low down on this guy while you were cleaning up your shit pile, Johnny."

No Nuts looked at Sid. "Fuck you."

"Parker says this security guard owes him some serious coin and it was his idea to take that bank in the first place."

"Credit union," No Nuts corrected him.

"What-the-fuck ever, Johnny. Are you with me?"

"Course I'm with you, Sid."

He grinned. "I told you this'd all work out, didn't I, old bean?"

"Well it ain't worked out yet," No Nuts reminded him.

"Not yet, but it will. Plus, we get to shoot this cocksucker that capped Bruiser."

No Nuts said he didn't care about that, said he never liked that asshole.

"Nobody did."

The Lexus was louder than ever, but Sid guaranteed No Nuts it was fine. Soon they'd find the money, and he'd buy another one.

"Yeah, but what if we don't find the money?"

"We'll find it, Johnny. I promise." No Nuts told Sid he had an idea that would fix everything, and Sid told him he couldn't wait to hear it.

"What if we go see the guard, we fix him up nice and proper. We tell Parker we made him talk, say all the security guard wanted was to kill Bruiser and be some hero. Say Bruiser was the one fuckin' the Mrs. We'll say it was *him* that was long-dickin' her."

Sid frowned. "You think we should tell Parker that Bruiser was long-dickin' the missus?"

"Trust me, Sid, it'll work." Sid turned to No Nuts with his mouth open, said, "So, to be clear, you want us to tell Parker this security guard, who owed him money, set this whole thing up just to kill Bruiser? That Bruiser was long-dickin' his wife, and the security guard just wanted to impress her? Is that what you want us to tell the boss, Johnny"

"Somethin' like that. He wanted to be a hero and eliminate his competition at the same time."

Sid was astounded. "That's not gonna work."

"And why not?"

"Why not? Well think about it, Johnny. What about his bloody wife? At some point she's gonna say she ain't been long-dicked by either one of 'em."

No Nuts shrugged and admitted he hadn't thought it through. "We'll kill her too."

Sid threw his hands up dramatically. "Well that's it then. Now you've gone and bloody lost it, I'll say. We can't just kill everybody, mate."

They rode in silence with the exception of the fender rubbing against the back tire.

Sid perked up. "What if we blame it on that bloke, Valentine? Say the guard had something going on the side with *him*. Make it look like they're in it together. What do ya think?"

When I opened my eyes, Frank was standing on my chest, licking my lips with his miniature Yorkshire tongue. I pushed him away instinctively, and the little bastard snapped at me. I remembered last night suddenly. I looked at the shotgun beside the couch; the .45 was there too.

Frank kept on barking, and I asked him what his problem was.

The phone rang as I stood up and peered out through the window at the ice-covered streets down below. I leaned over my desk and answered.

"Nick Valentine, Private Investigator."

It was Chief Caraway. Said he'd been calling all morning. He asked where I'd been.

I looked down at the morning wood stabbing through a hole in my boxers and told the Chief I'd been gathering information, running down leads. Told him I had my ear to the street, and he asked me what I'd come up with.

"Hang on a minute. I got a license plate number here somewhere." I rummaged through a pile of clothes on the floor until I found the number, then read it to him. Told him I thought it might be the man from the getaway truck.

"Great work, Nick."

I told him thanks. Assured him I'd been busting my ass, but I was just doing my part.

"I need you down here soon as you can, Nick."

I looked at the clock. Dead batteries, still. I needed to ask Doyle to get me a watch.

I nodded, told the Chief I was on my way, then I grabbed a couple of White Castle's from the mini and went to take my obligatory morning piss. Frank barked the whole time.

When I pulled up to the police station Ron was waiting for me in his car.

I asked him how he was doing.

He said he was good, told me to jump in with him. "Got a homicide to check out."

"Homicide?"

"I'll explain it on the way."

I shoved the shifter in park and laid a jacket over the shotgun. Just in case anyone felt meddlesome. Nevertheless, I couldn't imagine a safer place for a trashbag full of stolen money than the trunk of a former police car at a police station.

When I sat down in the passenger seat of his car, I entered a fog of cigarette smoke so impenetrable I thought I'd be forced to grab my chainsaw from the Vic and cut a path between Amish Ron and me. I ordered him to put his window down, and he laughed.

Ron exhaled, asked me was I sure I didn't want a cigarette?

I told him no thanks. But if I did chose to restart that terrible habit it sure as hell wouldn't be with one of those goddamn Winston's.

"Hey, what you got against Winston's?"

"Besides the fact they taste like a hobo's asshole? Nothing."

The Amishman laughed. Said that was a good one. He asked me about that license plate number I gave the Chief.

"Tracked it down through a source," I told him.

He nodded, said, "I can't wait to catch these guys."

Under different circumstances I'd applaud that kind of self-assurance, but his statement confirmed what I'd already suspected. He wouldn't give up easily.

"Glad to hear you're confident."

He shrugged. "This whole credit union thing is one big clusterfuck of epic proportions, Valentine."

I raised an eyebrow, encouraging him on.

"That security guard? He's dead."

I was taken aback. "Dead?"

Amish Ron was driving so slow I thought about jumping out and running on ahead to the crime scene. I glanced at the speedometer.

"Am I drivin' too slow for you, Nick?"

"No, I always like to drive about 37 myself."

"I hate this fucking snow," Ron said. "I try not to drive in it if I don't have to."

"That's right, you're not used to the snow. Your first car was a horse and buggy."

Ron looked up at the ceiling, laughed hard. Told me he knew sooner or later I was bound to make a horse joke.

I asked him if he missed it.

"What? Workin' my ass off for no money? Havin' no electricity? What's to miss?"

I couldn't argue with that logic. Being Amish sounded like a lot of work.

He got onto the interstate and opened her up to 52 mph. Slow enough we had a school bus pass us. I asked him about the security guard.

He said there wasn't much to know. The guy's name was Jason Baker. He asked me if that name rang any bells.

I told Ron I'd never heard of him as I worked out the details in my head.

"Let's get this straight," I began. "First, this guy, Norman Russo, he's..." I paused, "what, murdered? We know he didn't kill himself, right?"

Ron nodded.

"And now this security guard ends up dead the next day?"

"Exactly," Ron joined in. "Somebody's cleaning house, tying up loose ends."

"But why the security guard? Retaliation? You think

139

somebody's pissed off he shot up one of their crew? Cause I'd be happy if that was my crew."

Ron shrugged. Said, "Maybe." He asked me to elaborate.

"Well, maybe the guard was inside on this thing." I told Ron to bear with me. "So the guard smokes one of 'em in the back. That's less cash has to be drawn from the pile. And then, whoever set this up, kills the driver *and* the guard. Everybody who doesn't get shot makes three times as much and there's no witnesses."

Ron pulled a Winston loose and jammed it in his mouth. "There's a thought."

"It might also help explain that suicide note. The guard talks to the banker, he knows this guy's going through a rough divorce, he just wants to keep his house."

Ron was already ahead of me. "So he repeats that to whatever shit bum wrote the note, but then this guy who actually writes the note is too stupid and he fucks it up." I pictured the tweaker being too stupid and fucking it up.

I knew Bruiser was dead. I assumed the tweaker was dead. Now the security guard was dead. Parker assembled the heist with grandiose ambition, but he didn't count on Bruiser getting his back blown out through his chest. He never cared about doing it right, and he knew the police weren't stupid. He knew they wouldn't buy the suicide, but by the time they put everything together it would be too late. He was going to smoke the tweaker anyway, Bruiser too. They were disposable.

Sounds of the road filled the car, and something on the highway vibrated every quarter mile or so that I felt in my feet.

"Is there anything you're not tellin' me?" I asked.

He nodded and lit his smoke, told me there was something I outta know.

"What's that?"

He took a long drag, remembering to put down the window.

"Dye packs," Ron said, exhaling smoke. "That's the one thing that ties all of this together."

"Bank dye packs?" Had Doyle mentioned dye packs? I couldn't remember.

"Norman Russo collected the dye packs at the end of each night, locked them in a safe in his office. Safe's a combination, but he's the only one that's got it. Each morning he'd set 'em out again."

I told Ron I didn't know much about banks apart from the fact I didn't trust them.

He said he didn't know much about banks either, but he did know a thing or two about dye packs.

"Tellers have these packs by their station. If they get robbed, they slip 'em in with the money. When you make it out the door a remote signal sets 'em off."

"Then you're pretty much fucked," I said.

"Yeah, then you're fucked. But, in theory, if you eliminate the possibility of the dye packs being set out in the first place, you stand a good chance of getting away clean."

"As long as the security guard doesn't pound holes into your back."

"Yes, there's that."

"Whoever robbed the credit union knew Norman Russo set the dye packs out in the morning." I paused. "Only somebody with knowledge of their routine would know that."

"Somebody like the security guard."

Between the two of us we'd come up with a functioning hypothesis. We made the rest of the drive with the sound of highway as our third companion.

We got off Interstate 44 and drove into South County, to a middle-class neighborhood with typical ranch homes. We turned into a cul-de-sac, and I could see the last house on the left had two patrol cars and a meatwagon parked in the driveway. A familiar scene to both of us. Ron parked on the corner and lit up his smoke. He asked if I was ready.

When I stepped out of the car, the brisk air was revitalizing. I reeked of cigarette odor that covered me in a cloud of stench.

I followed him into the house, watched him shake a few hands. Nobody said much to me, which was fine. That's the way I like it.

Ron approached a tall black officer with a slim build who handed us each a pair of latex gloves and asked, "What do we have here?"

"This guy is fucked up, Ron."

Detective Beachy stepped inside the doorway, said, "Oh shit." But with his hint of Dutch accent, it sounded more like *sheeeit*.

I followed him through the doorway expecting a scene similar to the one at Norman Russo's, but that's not what I got.

"Where's his feet?" Ron wanted to know.

"Where's his hands?" I demanded.

The officer leaned back against the wall and gave us room.

Ron looked at the officer and said, "Well Clarence, I guess he must'a pissed somebody off."

"Aw, that shit is *nasty*. Look what the motherfuckers done to his head."

The victim's dismembered body was propped up in a corner minus hands or feet. Blood pooled in the ears, encompassed in raw blisters. The skin around the face had been beaten. It was swelled and bruised and dead.

Detective Beachy took a step forward, bent down.

The inside of the guard's ears were pallid and crusty with dried blood.

"This is interesting. It looks like scorched pus." He was

talking to an officer named Jim Jenkins as another plainclothes detective entered the room. He was tall, in good shape, like he knew his way around a gym. We shook hands; he said his name was Wyman.

Ron said, "His eardrums look like they've been burned out with cigarettes."

Clarence scrunched his face up tight, created wrinkles. "*Oh hail no!* Somebody fucked this cat up!"

If that was Clarence's professional opinion, I was inclined to agree with it. The Englishman was truly a ruthless cocksucker, the likes of which I'd never seen.

I pointed to deep grooves carved into the floor, filled with blood and fresh splinters.

"Here's where they chopped him up."

Ron took a close look, said, "They used an ax." That's what it looked like to me too, but I assumed he'd probably forgotten more about splitting wood than I'd ever learn. Given a choice, I would have used a chainsaw.

Ron walked back over to the body. He bent down and removed a business card with a set of tweezers.

"This is interesting." He held it up to the light. "What do you make of this, Nick?"

I would have recognized that card anywhere. It had my name on it.

"I've never seen this guy."

Ron stood up. Said he believed me, but I don't think he did.

We walked out into the living room and everything was in order; there was a wallet on the end table with the edge of a twenty poking out. It was easy to rule out robbery as a motive.

I walked into the kitchen and checked the fridge. I tried to keep my thoughts clean, but I knew those cocksuckers had been to my office. I kept a tray outside the door with a few cards in it. While I was sleeping they were out in the hall. If they'd suspected I had the money they would've kicked my door in and plugged me on the couch. Unless they were setting me up.

Detective Wyman walked past me with a cigar in his hand and stepped out into the backyard.

Ron nudged my shoulder. "What's goin' on here, Nick?"

I looked him in the eye and told him a God's honest lie.

"I have no fucking idea, Ron."

He began to speak, but his phone vibrated and he pulled it from the pocket of his jacket.

"Beachy."

He had a brief conversation with a dispatcher on the other end, thanked him and hung up.

He told me, "When they ran your plate number it came back to a car reported abandoned yesterday just down the road. Montgomery's Steak House."

I told him I knew the place.

"Good," he said. "You can drive."

I pulled onto Lindbergh, jumped into the hammer lane, and held the accelerator on the standard police-issue Impala to the floor.

"Good God, slow down."

I told Amish Ron not to light up that cancer stick in his hand and I'd see what I could do about my driving.

Ron said he'd hold off on the smoke if I'd come clean with him. Was there anything I was holding back?

I told him I'd never seen that prick back there in my life. I'd never seen the banker before either.

"All I've done from the beginning is try and find that money. I've asked around, I even banged a few heads. I did what I had to do to get answers."

"But you work outside the same laws I'm trying to protect."

"I do it so you don't have to."

Ron went silent; I wondered what kinds of thoughts were going through his Amish head.

He told me I could drive as fast as I wanted, but he was having a smoke. Was I sure I didn't want one?

"Stop trying to corrupt me," I scolded.

He shrugged, told me I really should relax. Something I was well aware of.

I needed alcohol as soon as possible. Maybe a painkiller could be arranged.

I pulled into Montgomery's, and Ron pointed to the car.

"That white one in the back." It was just as Doyle described.

Ron got out first as I slipped a single Oxycontin out of my pocket and placed it in my mouth, *incognito*. I'd spent the last few minutes working up enough spit to carry it down the pipe. I'd gotten used to the taste long ago and it was quite tolerable. Xanax, on the other hand, was a different story. Those required half a Corona, minimum.

We did a visual inspection. Ron said the car was registered to a Tim Kelly.

"Never trust a man with two first names." It was advice I got from Big Tony once, but apparently it went over Ron's head.

"What do you know about this guy?"

I told Ron I didn't know jack shit. Said I'd gotten the number, heard he might've been the driver.

"It's probably a dead end."

He looked up at me, said, "It's not."

"Oh really?"

"Had a report of a white Buick leaving the scene." Ron tapped on the trunk lid, asked me if I'd pop it.

I couldn't help but notice he expected full disclosure from me but had no problem dispersing his own information whenever he deemed it necessary or appropriate. When I sat down, the headliner was in my face, and I had to wrestle with it as I leaned over to the glove box and popped the trunk.

"See anything back there?" I yelled.

Ron said there was nothing but a toolbox with a roll of aluminum foil inside. "There's not even a spare tire." He asked me what kind of idiot drove around without a spare tire?

I agreed wholeheartedly, but didn't bother to tell him I was one of those idiots without a spare tire. All I had in my own trunk was a spare beer cooler, and a Stihl Wood Boss. Oh, and a trashbag full of stolen money two people died for—including that poor bastard who had his eardrums used as an ashtray.

I parted ways with Amish Ron and stopped at the nearest gas station for a cold beverage. I filled the Vic up with 93 octane and grabbed a bottle of rum, a bag of ice, and a five-pound sack of the best dog food in the house. Frank hadn't eaten a solid meal since yesterday morning, and he was getting pissed off.

I loaded up the Vic and tore out of the parking lot sideways. I jumped on the interstate, popped open a forty-ounce Budweiser and drank it still wrapped in the bag. I waited for the pill to kick in, but Oxy's are designed for *time-release.*

It took forever if you did it the old-fashioned way, as I'd been forced to do. I needed to smash up another 20 as soon as I had the chance. Through trial and error, I'd discovered snorting was the preferred method of ingestion. A necessary requirement if you wanted to receive the full effect like a shotgun blast to the brain.

I refused to call Big Tony even though I knew I should.

Maybe he and Doyle had already skipped town. I hoped for their sake they had. Things were out of control, and I was pretty sure I'd have to start killing people soon. Not because I wanted to keep the money, but because killing them was the right thing to do. These pricks were sticking lit cigarettes in people's earholes. What kind of sick asshole thought of something like that?

I turned off onto Blackmore Road and finished the last drop of my Bud. I tossed the can on the floorboard between the leftover bowl of chili from Cowboy Roy's and a bottle of *Hot Damn* cinnamon schnapps. On closer inspection, it appeared to still have a few good drinks left in the bottom.

I parked in the same place I usually did and decided to leave the cash in the trunk. I wouldn't be there long, and I'd draw suspicion if my neighbors saw me constantly hauling trash up and down the stairs.

I got to the top step and looked at the empty tray where my cards used to be. I shook my head. Those cocksuckers were trying to set me up.

I unlocked the door, turned the handle, and stepped in. Frank wasn't waiting on the other side, scratching and dancing.

I pushed my way into the room with a bag of ice, a bottle of rum, and five pounds of the best gas station dog food I could find.

English Sid was sitting on the couch I used for a bed with his feet propped up on the box I used as a coffee table.

I did my best to conceal my shock, but the bombshell of him sitting there so comfortably dealt me an earth-shattering blow like a sucker punch. I said, "Good afternoon cocksucker."

The Englishman grinned.

"Ah, Valentine. I always heard you had a good sense of humor." His British accent was thicker than I'd anticipated.

"Then I'm sure you've also heard I've got a bad attitude, a short temper, and a long cock."

Sid tilted his head back and laughed.

"Valentine, Valentine. What're we goin' to do with you?"

"Well if your thinkin' about stickin' a Marlboro in my ear you're gonna hafta kill me first." I noticed he said *we*, but I held his gaze. I wasn't giving him the satisfaction of seeing me sweat.

"Thought you'd get a kick out of that, mate." Sid turned his head sharply to the left and looked at me hard, reading my strained face from the comfort of my couch.

"Where's the money dickhead?"

I was still holding the ice, the rum, and the dog food. There was no way to reach my .45.

I gave him a hard look back, asked him what money he was talking about. *The credit union money?* I told him I was working the case.

"Course you're workin' the case. You're also workin' the street with Fat Tony and that other fuck that robbed Joe Parker."

"Joe, who?"

Sid stood up quick, the expression on his face abruptly shifting from bad to worse.

"Don't get cute with me, ya cunt! I'll cut your bloody ears off and show 'em to ya, Valentine."

I told him to go ahead and try it.

"Oh, you're a real tough guy aintchya? Saw what you did to that poor bloke back at the club."

I shrugged. "Guess there was just something about that mustache."

"Oh really? You didn't like that?" He looked behind me. "Hey, didja hear that Johnny? Valentine here didn't like that mustache." His eyes cut into me; I could tell he wasn't going to play this game much longer.

148

A voice came from the kitchen area but my eyes were bonded to the Englishman with adhesive.

"I kinda liked that mustache."

I dropped the ice and the dog food quick and tossed the bottle to Sid. I jumped to my left and reached for my gun, but Sid was faster than I'd expected.

He charged me, we collided, and our bodies hit the floor. He got in a few good blows, told me to calm down.

I was pinned to the floor, but I'd been in worse situations. The .45 was underneath me, pushing hard into the small of my back.

"Where's the money, motherfucker?" Sid drove a hard fist deep into my cheek, and I felt it.

"Where's the money?" he repeated, slammed me again.

My ears rang; my face was hot and tight, blood ran thin under the surface of my battered skin. I told him I didn't have the money. "Look at this shithole. Does it look like I've got any money?"

I saw his fist come again, and I threw my head into it. His knuckles rapped on the top of my skull and bones broke.

"*Fuck!*" Sid screamed. He drilled me with a straight left to the jaw that I never saw coming, and my head bounced off the floor. Sid smashed me again with another left, but there was nowhere for me to go, so I took it.

He screamed, "My bloody hand. You motherfucker."

I tried to turn into his punches with the top of my head, but I was losing consciousness.

My mouth filled with blood. Time slowed down, and the only noise I heard was white static. I couldn't see anything but blotches of cold, penetrating darkness pushing down on me.

He put a gun to my face, pushed it into my forehead, then leaned down and put all his weight on it.

"It's real simple. I'll shoot you in the fucking face right now if you don't give me the money, Valentine."

"Just as long as you don't burn me with cigarettes."

Sid continued to belittle me in between blows.

"You—stupid—fucking—Americans."

My eyes were swelling shut. My head was sideways, pushed into the floor. My only real view was the bottle of *Ron Bacardi Superior Rum*. Then a big pair of dress shoes came into focus.

"Ask him where the money is, Johnny."

"Where's the fucking money asshole?"

When I looked up it took me a minute to realize what I was seeing.

Sid grabbed me by the hair, pulled my head off the carpet, forced me to look over.

"Get a good luck at No Nuts."

I blinked, squinted. The one he called No Nuts was standing in my kitchen area. When he stepped toward me I realized he had Frank Sinatra stuffed in a blender. The big yellow blender Frank didn't like.

"*Frank!*"

Sid looked over at No Nuts and laughed.

"I think we've got his attention now, Johnny."

"*You motherfuckers!*" With every raw fragment of strength I could generate, I drove my forehead into Sid's nose and crushed it flat against his cheek. I'd almost managed to throw him off, but he rammed the butt of his handgun into my face.

I went out cold, swallowing blood.

I couldn't see anything; I disappeared into a world where time slowed. I heard voices in the distance, whispers and echoes distorted.

I blinked slowly with my right eye, took in what I could in hasty ambiguous flashes. I couldn't feel my face. The

Englishman was on my chest, crushing me. Driving the wind out of my burning lungs. I struggled for every breath I could get. Everything slowed until time turned still and motionless.

I heard them in the darkness as they talked about who had the money, how the three of us each took a cut. I opened the absolute bare minimum amount of eyelid required to see. The rest of my life depended on the next few seconds.

The 12-gauge lay to my right, next to the couch where I'd left it, hidden between two boxes that served as end tables. There were advantages to living in a dump; a shotgun could stay hidden among the newspapers and debris.

I clenched and unclenched my fist slowly, moving my fingers to within inches of the pistol grip.

I was dead inside, couldn't move. Gray shapes floated in front of my eyes. But when I thought about Frank, my body moved again, and my palm touched the cool wood of the gunstock.

Sid looked down into my face but couldn't see my hand locked on the pistol grip.

"I think this prick's awake," he said to No Nuts.

"Anybody in there, Valentine?" He knocked on my forehead with the hand that wasn't broken. "What? Nothing smart to say? No more wise arse?"

I opened my eye. Tried to talk, but the words came hard. *"Fuck the Beatles."*

Even through the small part of my eye that worked I could see the British cocksucker do a double take as the wind was sucked from his lungs unexpectedly.

"Awe, now that's beautiful Valentine. Oh, you really are

151

a crazy bastard now aren'tchya? Did'ya hear what he said, Johnny? *Fuck the Beatles*, he says."

I blinked as blood ran into my eye, and Sid told me as strange as it might sound coming from an Englishman, he couldn't stand the fucking Beatles either. He said, "I'm more of a Def Leppard fan myself."

I couldn't breath; I coughed and fought for air.

"See, No Nuts and me, we been thinkin'. What you say this bloody wanker has the money in the trunk of his bloody car?"

To my left stood No Nuts next to my oversize margarita blender on the counter. Somehow most of my Yorkshire terrier fit inside. No Nuts was holding the lid down tight with one hand, and Frank wasn't barking.

I had one shot to make. Blow the Englishman off my chest and through the window or shoot that fat son-of-a-bitch that had Frank in such an awkward predicament.

Sid gave the order and made my choice easy.

"Go ahead Johnny. Grind that little fucker up."

As No Nuts reached for the button I pulled the shotgun out, brought the short barrel down in front of Sid's nose, and fired toward the top of No Nuts' head.

BOOM! The short barrel belched fire, and the pattern spread quick, caught No Nuts in the face and shoulder. The ceiling above him exploded and collapsed on top of him.

Sid dove off my chest and rolled out the door into the hall.

Finally, I could breathe; I sucked the air in greedily.

A portion of the door detonated like a wood bomb as Sid fired, and jagged splinters of debris flew through the air.

I rolled over to my side, brought the gun up, and fired a round out into the hallway. The glass exploded in the middle of the door that displayed my name and rained down, covering the grimy carpet in diamond shards.

No Nuts couldn't stand. He stumbled toward me, bent over and bleeding plentifully on the floor.

I pulled myself onto my stomach and drove my elbow in the carpet like I was plowing earth, pulling myself forward. The shotgun swung in my right hand, moving from the hallway to the kitchen. I thought I had two shots left.

"Johnny!" Sid was blaring from the hallway.

My ears were useless; my vision dead in one eye.

I tried to speak. "Frank!"

No Nuts fell against my cardboard counter and the blender tumbled to the floor. It grinded for a moment, and Frank gave out a horrifying screech. Then it stopped.

I tried standing up and fell out the door on one knee, shotgun in my hand. No Nuts shoved past me, but I righted myself and stayed conscious long enough to make it down the steps.

I stepped into the scorching light and racked the 12-gauge with one hand while I held the left out for balance. The car pulled from the alley and raced toward me.

I staggered onto Blackmore and blasted the side passenger door, then blew out the back window.

Empty.

I tossed the shotgun on the ground and drew the .45 from behind my back, threw my arm around to the side and started firing rounds. At least two in the trunk, another one passed straight through. I stumbled back toward the sidewalk and collapsed in the snow.

S id held the pedal down with all his weight, like he was trying to shove his foot through the floorboard. The big engine screamed, and the tires left scars across the parts of

Blackmore road not covered in snow as the Lexus was peppered with shotgun pellets.

The back window shattered as a round from a .45 passed between them, punched a hole in the windshield, then took a small chunk of metal off the hood. More lead pounded into the trunk.

"*Fuck!*" No Nuts screamed as he slid down to the floorboard. Holes blasted through the door and shrapnel carved into his right leg.

"I been hit, Sid!" He fumbled with his gun.

No Nuts looked into the passenger side mirror with caution as a thick trail of blood ran down his cheek onto his chest. His face was shredded; one of his eyes was shot out.

More gunshots followed, then a bullet struck the dashboard. Nervously, without thinking, Johnny fired out the window without putting it down.

It burst into pieces, spraying his already-peppered face with new shards.

"Fer fuck's sake." Sid slid the Lexus to the left with the ease of a seasoned wheelman.

"Put down the window you stupid bastard."

But No Nuts wasn't listening. He fired out the window into a vacant lot and hit a minivan, the bullet drilling into the cheap sheetmetal.

"Johnny, he's *behind us* you dumbfuck!"

Sid couldn't move his right hand. He had a boxer's fracture of the metacarpal bone; it was swollen twice the size it should've been. His nose was an inferno of hot throbbing pain; he used his mouth to breath. Both eyes were starting to darken nicely.

Sid looked over at No Nuts, and he knew Johnny was in a bad way. His t-shirt looked like it'd been soaked in red paint. One eye looked like it was gone; his face was filled with lead pellets. His short round forehead lay open to the skull; part of his cheek was missing. Sid didn't want to stare.

"Aw, fuck! You still with me Johnny?"

But Johnny wasn't with him.

Sid barreled through an alley, barely missing a taxi, then hung a very hard right onto Broadway, crossed two lanes of light traffic, blew through a red light, and made a quick left behind a brick building some asshole was just letting sit there and go to waste.

No Nuts always said it would make a good bakery.

Sid parked the Lexus and took a close look at his partner.

"I'm done, Sid. I'm done." No Nuts was getting hard to understand.

"No, you'll be fine Johnny. Couple uh aspirin oughta fix ya right up."

"I think I slat my pants, Sid," No Nuts slurred. Part of his cheek was missing. There was a gaping hole in the corner of his mouth where his upper lip connected to his lower. Open folds of skin leaked blood and spit.

Johnny's tongue kept sliding out of his face.

"I. . . slat. . . my. . .shelf . . .Thid."

Sid had Johnny's arms; he pulled him up in his seat, but it felt like his arm would pull free. There was too much slack. Everything felt loose, unfastened.

"You *shat* your pants?" Sid tried to take Johnny's mind off the hole in his face.

"Or did you *shit* your pants? Because I believe *shat* may actually be used as the past tense in this situation."

No Nuts groaned and bled heavily. Sid tried to distance himself from the thought of his Lexus now covered in vomit *and* blood.

"Gotta go now. You with me Johnny? We gotta get the fuck outta here."

Sid tore across the lot in reverse, and Johnny fell forward and crashed hard into the dashboard, leaving fresh smears of blood.

"Well fuck, Johnny," Sid yelled.

Johnny yelled something back, but it was impossible to understand.

Sid caught a green light as his phone rang.

"It's Parker."

After they murdered the security guard they had set things into play. They went back, woke up Parker, told him Valentine was involved. How far they didn't know. Said they had a plan to fuck him good. They'd pay him a visit; see if he had the money.

On the third ring he slid the lock across and said, "It's done."

Mr. Parker stayed silent for a second, but Sid could hear him breathing heavily through his nose, as was his habit in tense situations. Sid flipped the blinker and switched lanes. Johnny No Nuts just groaned and bled.

"*The eagle has landed*?"

"Uh, yeah. The eagle landed."

Mr. Parker was obsessed with spy novels and always managed to speak in codes, no matter ridiculous they might sound.

"I trust you have the package?"

"Negative sir, we do not have the package." Sid felt like a fool.

"Where's No Nuts?"

Sid looked over to his right at Johnny, who had his back up against the door, staring at him. You could see his bottom set of teeth through his cheek.

"He's right here." Sid held the phone toward Johnny, but his face made a grotesque sucking sound.

"You tell that short fat fuck he better not have fucked anything up, Sid, you hear me?"

That was Mr. Parker's way of joking, but Johnny wasn't laughing. Just slobbering and bleeding and letting his tongue slide through that hole.

"I'm *dyin'*," Johnny whispered.

Sid just shrugged his shoulders, shook his head from side to side.

Johnny sat up a little straighter and yelled something useless. Blood was starting to pour from that main hole now, and Sid didn't like the looks of it.

"Well, what the fuck happened back there, Sid?" Mr. Parker demanded. "I told you to keep an eye on that retard." Mr. Parker's way of telling Sid that *he* was responsible. "All you had to do was get the money."

"You mean *the package*," Sid corrected him.

Before Parker could respond, the Lexus was rammed from behind by a white Chevy van that said Drysdale's Electric. The impact ripped the steering wheel from his hands, and the car swerved hard to the left, bouncing off a red Dodge truck.

Sid regained control and Johnny went back into the dashboard, then onto the floorboard.

The van came again, got along the driver's side, and somebody waved a handgun.

Sid nailed the brakes and swerved hard. The Lexus slammed into a Nissan Maxima, and fresh glass broke from their driver's window and filled the inside of the Lexus.

Sid rammed the Nissan again and sent it to the shoulder. "*They found us, Johnny!*" But Johnny didn't care. He was too busy dying.

Sid hammered the accelerator, and the Lexus bogged down. The rear bumper was dragging the highway as the van picked up speed. The Lexus could only withstand one, maybe two more hits before it would shit out completely.

Quickly, and without warning, Sid cut the wheels hard to the right, and the engine raced, the tires screeched, and he clipped the front bumper of a baby-shit green Ford Focus with what used to be the rear bumper of the Lexus, crossed into the far right lane and plunged off the shoulder. The pummeled Lexus slid down the steep bank sideways through pockets of gray winter snow, then righted.

The electrical van got stuck in traffic and couldn't follow Sid's crazed exit.

Sid kept the gas pedal smashed as the car burst through the remnants of a chain link fence, jumped a curb, then blended in with traffic on Charbonneau Boulevard before taking a left.

No Nuts asked Sid if he was gonna die.

"Course not, Johnny."

Johnny coughed, spit blood into his hand. He held it towards Sid.

"Well fuck me, Johnny!" Sid gave him a firm shove and No Nuts fell into the door.

"Have ya gone bloody mad?"

Johnny was breathing hard but getting it under control.

"We never shoulda took that money, Sid."

"What're you talkin' about Johnny? Course we shoulda."

"Easy for you to say."

Sid asked him if he wanted to go to a hospital.

No Nuts laughed, said it wasn't gonna help.

"Listen Johnny, I'm goin' ta fix you right up, ok?"

No Nuts nodded. "Where we goin'?"

"Remember that girl from the club I was bangin'? She only lives maybe two miles away."

Sid looked down at his phone on the floorboard; he wondered if Parker was still listening. Everything was fucked up. His hand, his nose, *his Lexus*. Plus there was Johnny's face and whatever else. He looked over at No Nuts and told him to hang in there. No Nuts gave him a single thumb up.

Sid was sure they'd lost the van. He never saw it get off the highway; there'd been nothing in his rear-view but flying snow and remnants of a chain link fence that dragged behind the car for several hundred feet.

"We're here, Johnny," he announced.

Sid parked in the driveway next door, in case they were followed, and did his best to pull No Nuts from the car without pulling his shoulder off his body.

"Her car's probably in the garage, less she ain't here. That'd be good news, huh mate?"

Sid dragged No Nuts around to the back door where she kept a hidden key. He set him up in a kitchen chair and fixed him a Bloody Mary, which seemed like the right drink for the moment.

"You're going to be all right," Sid assured him without conviction. "Now, let's see about fixin' you up proper."

Sid looked at No Nuts in the light and knew it was only a matter of time before he was done. It would be a bittersweet way to end a partnership. They'd killed together. Cut up bodies together. No Nut's demise would leave Sid without a dependable colleague. But on the other hand, Sid was confident Johnny's share of the money would fill any emotional void created by his departure.

"You gonna take care of me, Sid?" His words came slow, requiring vast effort.

Sid promised he would, told Johnny he'd be right back. He made his way down the hallway to the medicine cabinet. He knew with all of Angie's piercings she was bound to have top-notch first aid supplies.

He returned with a wet washcloth, a bottle of rubbing alcohol, gauze, and a roll of gray duct tape.

No Nuts' good eye blinked wildly when he saw the duct tape.

He began to protest, but Sid shut him down. Told him to chill out. Said he was gonna do him right and proper. As No Nuts tried to take a drink of Bloody Mary, the Englishman dumped a big splash of alcohol into the holes on Johnny's face.

No Nuts came up off the chair quickly and misplaced his balance. He stumbled backwards, knocked a vase with flowers off the table and it crashed to the linoleum.

"Well watch the table then you cunt!"

No Nuts sat down on top of the cheap kitchen table. One of the legs buckled under his weight, but did not break. He screamed while blood and alcohol poured from numerous wounds.

"Well, ya just *had* to go and break the bloody centerpiece you goofy bastard, now didn't ya?"

"Fuck you, Thid! And fuck tha thennerpieth! I'm dyin over here."

Sid did his best to decipher No Nuts' juicy slurrings. "Well at least have a little dignity about it, ya fuck. Show some respect. That centerpiece really tied the room together."

No Nuts told Sid he could go back to England and fuck the Queen's dog in the arse. He asked him why he threw that stinging shit in his face like he did.

"I'm just tryin' to help ya Johnny. Thought it'd be easier if you didn't see it comin'."

No Nuts shook his head. Said, "I'm gonna kill Valentine. I'm gonna kill that cockthucker."

Sid nodded in approval. He patted No Nuts on his good shoulder, told him *that's the spirit*. Told him soon he'd be good as new. Sid went over to the fridge and made No Nuts another drink.

When Sid came back, No Nuts told him they never checked the trunk for the money.

"Yeah, I know Johnny. Didn't exactly have time on account of you getting shot in the face and all."

No Nuts took a deep breath and groaned. He exhaled powerfully, and Sid watched his cheek open and close like a tent flap.

"We're gonna need to do something about that cheek of yours, old boy."

Johnny said he knew. He nodded pathetically, asked Sid how he looked.

"Well, ain't nobody goin' ta confuse you for George Clooney anytime soon, but it ain't that bad."

No Nuts sipped on that drink, but he had to turn his head to the right or tomato juice would run out of the holes. He told Sid he wished he had a painkiller.

Sid told No Nuts he'd just have to tough it out. He reminded No Nuts he wasn't the only one hurting. "Look at my damn nose, Johnny." Then he raised his right hand. "Look at this, it's bloody broken."

"Geth we both got fucked up, Thid."

"Yeah Johnny, I guess we did."

A gust of wind picked up a loose piece of siding and slapped it up against the house, and No Nuts jumped.

"Relax," Sid said. "It always does that."

He took a seat beside No Nuts, and they finished their drinks.

"This little game we're playing with Joe Parker ain't gonna last much longer, Johnny. We gotta find these guys tonight, get the money, then get the fuck outta this city for good." He asked No Nuts if he was ready.

No Nuts finished up the last drop of tomato juice and told Sid to get to it.

Sid tore off a few pieces of duct tape, which varied in length. He ripped a few pieces up the middle too and stuck the edges to the end of the table.

"Now this may smart a little bit, Johnny." Sid tried to clean him up with the washcloth, but he wasn't having much luck. He scrubbed for a minute, then he started using sections of the tape to patch Johnny's face together.

When he was finished there was duct tape across Johnny's cheek, ear, and nose. He could barely open his mouth enough to speak. Sid also taped No Nuts shoulder solid to his body by wrapping the tape around his back, up under his other arm, then back across to his shoulder. A few more times and No Nuts felt much better. Stiffer, a little tighter, but at least it didn't feel like his fucking shoulder was going to fall off.

He said he had to piss. Maybe he'd finally worked up the courage to look in the mirror. He asked Sid to make him another drink, said he'd be right back.

"Sure, Johnny." Sid made a drink for each of them.

The back door opened suddenly, and Sid eyeballed his burner on the table. It was Angie and some guy who looked familiar but Sid couldn't place. The guy was holding a burner of his own.

"Don't do it, buddy," the stranger yelled.

Sid stopped and tried to throw his hands up, but he was holding the glasses. "Calm down, calm down. Angie, it's me."

"Of course it's you, *asshole*! You leave me, don't talk to me for two months, then you just come over and break into my fucking house!"

"I didn't break in, darlin'. I used the key."

She looked at the glasses in his hands. "*And you help yourself to my booze?*"

"I was thirsty."

"Oh, fuck you!" she screamed.

Sid looked at the guy with the gun.

He looked like he could handle himself, but he was anxious. He'd be easy to overpower if Sid caught him off guard.

"Aren't you gonna introduce us, love?" He nodded at the new guy.

"You don't worry 'bout who I am, boy."

Her hair was wet. She was wearing loose sweatpants and a man's t-shirt. She smelled like mango.

"This is Bill," she said. "He lives next door."

Sid mentioned the wet hair, asked, "Is your shower broken, love?"

"I'm seein' Bill now, *you pig!*"

Bill started getting loud. He pointed hard with the gun.

"You parked your car in my driveway, jackoff! She got outta the shower'n she seen it. Told me it was yours. I done called the law on ya."

"Now why'd you have to go and do a thing like that for Bill?" Sid shook his head from side to side.

"Angie," Sid began, "just lemme go. Lemme go and I'll just be on me way." He moved to set the drinks down.

"Oh, fuck you. You're goin' to jail, asshole." If Bill ever noticed Sid had two drinks, he failed to recognize the significance.

Sid bit his lip, shrugged. Said they shoulda let him go.

"Johnny?"

No Nuts stepped out from the hallway and started shooting.

His right arm was taped solid and he had to use his left, something he'd never done before. He was aiming for Bill, but the first shot tore a hole through the stripper's chest, and she died on her feet. The second shot blew a chunk of wood off the doorframe. He aimed with the eye that still worked.

Bill froze, unaccustomed to the weight of the gun. He pointed at No Nuts and fired, but he never took the safety off. He fumbled with it as No Nuts charged him, running funny with half his body held together by duct tape.

Bill turned to run as two bullets punctured his back. One hammered through his shoulder and lodged against his spine. The other passed through his chest and struck a wall next to the backdoor.

He fell on his stomach and chunks of drywall landed on his back. No Nuts got close and blasted one finishing round into his mess of dark bushy hair, and the force at such close range lifted up Bill's head and slammed what was left back to the ground in a burst of blood, bone, and floor tile.

Sid took a drink and told Johnny that was pretty good shootin'. "Five bullets for two people, from only six feet away."

"Fuck you and you're welcome."

But Sid couldn't understand anything No Nuts said by that point.

They fled the scene, each with a gun in one hand and a Bloody Mary in the other. They couldn't leave them behind with their prints on them. Not that it mattered. They'd both touched too many things. That got Sid thinking. It wasn't too late to clean up this mess.

Sid stopped running, told No Nuts they couldn't leave things like they were. Said he had to go back to the garage. He knew there was five gallons worth of gas. Said he outta know, he was the bloke who cut the grass all summer. "I'm gonna torch the place, Johnny. Just wait for me in the car."

I felt cold snow against my face as someone grabbed me by the shoulders. There was a voice I couldn't see asking me if I was okay. I looked up into the sun that blinded me, told whoever was on the other end of that voice to help me to my feet.

I still had the .45 in my hand. I scanned the ground for my shotgun.

"Whoa, take it easy, man. Take it easy. *I can't believe that shit!* You okay?"

"Shotgun."

"Just hang on buddy; ain't you like a cop or something?"

My eyes opened and closed heavily.

The guy holding me up lived down the street. I'd seen him around. He drove a red Ford F-150 pickup with a camper just a tad off in color. Sometimes he'd walk up to the corner mart in the evenings, walk back with a bottle of wine and an ice cream.

He said his name was Clyde Kirby. He asked me again if I was a cop. His adrenaline was pumping; he was shaken up.

"What the fuck just happened, man?"

I walked forward and picked the shotgun up out of the snow. Clyde kept telling me to relax, said the cops were on their way.

I thought about Frank suddenly and made a run for the stairs, took them two at a time. I ran through the door and found him to my left, lying on his side. His lower half was still stuffed in the blender. I dropped the guns and fell to the ground. He wasn't moving, but he was alive. When I tried to pull him free, he started squealing. My hands froze. I couldn't do it. There was blood inside the blender and a shitload of hair. I whispered to him, struggled to pull him free. A wad of his fur was wrapped tightly in the blades, and his shriek made my ears bleed. As delicately as possible, I pulled him loose. He yelped and whimpered. I told him again it'd be okay. Promised I'd make them pay.

When I lifted him free one of his little paws stayed in the bottom of the blender.

"*Jesus Christ!*" Clyde was standing in the room with lines of shock etched deep across his face. "My God, son, what happened in this room?"

"I just got hit by a couple of thugs."

"What about your dog? *Was he in that blender?*"

Considering the circumstances, it was a legitimate question. But how do you tell a neighbor you barely know that a couple of cocksuckers just put your dog in a margarita blender because they were looking for a trashbag full of stolen money?

I rummaged through a box and grabbed a handful of 3-inch turkey loads for the shotgun and threw them in the leftover White Castle bag from the other night. I grabbed a bottle of Jim Beam from the same box. I'd made it a general rule to keep my ammunition and my alcohol within reach for emergencies such as this.

My vision all but returned in my left eye, but the right was still ridiculously swollen and full of blood. I moved my jaw around, and it didn't feel broken. I thought about Frank.

I grabbed the White Castle bag and handed it to Clyde, told him to follow me to the Vic. I scooped up Frank and what was left of his paw and wrapped him tight in a dishtowel. He stopped yelping, then he stopped moving altogether.

"Hang in there you little son-of-a-bitch."

With the other hand I picked up the shotgun and ran from the room, careful not to fall with Frank in my arms.

I hit the key, and the engine roared to life. I pumped the pedal twice to make the glass packs rumble, dropped it in *D*, held it to the floor as I cut the wheel, then spun that bad motherfucker completely around in the middle of Blackmore Road.

The Vic took turns fishtailing from left to right through sections of mixed ice and dry pavement until it finally caught traction. I ordered Frank to stay with me. I kept one hand on the bloody dishtowel that covered him.

I had to get him to the Animal Hospital off Big Bend, and I didn't know how much time he had.

I wondered how bad No Nuts was hit. It looked like I'd blown the top of his face off. I'd done my best to aim high and prayed like hell I didn't hit Frank. The irony of possibly killing him myself, in a failed attempt to save him from the blender, was not lost on me.

Amish Ron was going to shit himself when he found out what happened. He'd never believe me now. I knew there were already cops back at my place, and Clyde was telling stories.

Everything happened so fast that I had to wonder how much Clyde saw. Then I remembered the Englishman's broken hand, and I smirked.

I raced across the hospital lot and parked up close by the entrance. I yanked the key out of the ignition and grabbed Frank. I pulled my shirt down over the .45 and ran up to the front, kicked the door open. I told the attractive young girl at the desk I was a detective and this was my K-9 unit, asked her to cease all other functions at once and operate on Frank as if he were the President of the United States.

I handed Frank to the girl, and her gorgeous face dropped when she saw all the blood.

"Oh my God! What happened?"

I hadn't considered such a question so I told her the first thing that came to my mind.

"He was injured in the line of duty."

"Oh my God!" she exclaimed again. "Poor thing. He's really a police dog?"

She looked skeptical.

I told her of course he was a police dog. Narcotics.

"Poor thing," she repeated. "He's so tiny."

I agreed Frank was small for a Yorkshire, but I assured her that he was still a force to be reckoned with.

An older gentleman walked by in a white coat, glasses pushed down to the end of his nose. I grabbed him by the arm. "You a vet?"

He tried to pull away, but I wouldn't turn him loose.

"Are you?"

"Well yes," he growled.

"This is a crisis," I declared, and I told him we were dealing with a police emergency. Said I'd be back in the morning, and I made it clear in no uncertain terms Frank had better be alive and kicking with all fours, and not just three and a half.

I left the hospital and took a shot of Jim Beam from the bottle just as soon as I found the car. I loaded up the shotgun and turned up the heat. I couldn't stand to see Frank like that. I took another drink as I rummaged through the glove box for any painkillers. My face was swelling up; the skin around my eye was tight and filled with blood.

I felt my guts begin to smolder, and I knew that bourbon fire was on its way. Slow at first, but then it would come on strong like it always did.

Finally, I felt a bottle of something I hoped was stronger than Tylenol, pushed at it until I had it trapped in a corner and it stopped moving. I sat up and read the bottle. Percocet, a personal favorite of mine. It would do quite nicely.

I wasn't sure about my next move. I didn't know where to find Sid and No Nuts. Didn't know where to find Big Tony or Doyle. The one thing I *did* know was I needed to get back to my apartment and start answering questions. But maybe I should get a drink first and think about that. It was still early enough to catch Happy Hour at a little hole in the wall I knew just a mile or two down the road. I took a healthy drink of Beam as I left the parking lot.

I parked the Vic in front of a dirty battered shithole called the Queen of Hearts. The kind of place where the girls from the better titty bars across the river end up after they lost whatever it was they once had. This was the end of the line, home to fractured dreams and failed ambitions. The girls were a little heavier, and they had to wear g-strings, but the beer was just as cold and the drive was half as far.

I scanned the glove box for any more medication that may have escaped my attention. I knew I hadn't given the Perc's enough time to do their job, but my face was sending out violent shockwaves of excruciating pain.

One final belt of Jim Beam finished off the bottle, and I tossed it behind the seat. I tried to avoid my reflection in the mirror as I got out and walked across the lot.

I walked through the door and kept my head down, pushed ahead to the bar.

I got lucky, found an open seat at the end, and I did my very best to ignore the questioning looks of those around me. I told the barmaid I needed two Coronas and a White Russian.

"Is that all?"

"Better throw in a shot of Knob Creek just to be safe."

"Do I know you?" I saw her face search my face with curious amusement.

"Doubt it."

She contemplated my order. "Well, you expectin' company?"

I told her I was, then turned my back to the bar. Even in my current physical state I scanned the immediate surroundings for the best the Queen had to offer. I prepared to endure what was sure to be a painfully substandard striptease, performed to the appalling beat of music that should've never been recorded.

The sturdy dancer on the stage moved her body slowly against a pole that seemed to give an inch in each direction when she grinded. It looked like it might come unbolted from the roof at any minute.

"Here ya go, hon."

The barmaid returned with a full tray and I thanked her, left a twenty on the bar, and walked to a private table to drink alone.

The first Corona helped put out the fire created by the bourbon. The second Corona left me wanting more. I slammed the Caucasian. I slammed the Knob.

As I opted for a refill, the dancer from the stage walked up to me and told me I looked like I'd had a pretty bad day.

I asked what could make her say such a thing.

She laughed a little too deeply, and I heard the phlegm inside her lungs break loose and move about. As close as she was, I started noticing her flaws. Her skin was stretched and worn. The top of each ass cheek was broad enough to use as a ledge to set my drinks. But to be honest, she had a great smile, and I've always thought nice teeth were important.

I touched her gently on the shoulder and nudged her to the right, just a step, so she was out of the light, a strategic move that rendered her far more attractive than she was only moments before. I took a step closer, told her I liked the way she wore those pasties. I asked her if she wanted to come out to the Vic. Said I had plans for her.

"What kind of plans?" She smiled at me behind a nervous glance, and then I smiled. Let my eyes wander up and down her stout body.

When she stepped into the light, I pushed her back into the shadows, knowing this would go better for the both of us if I could pretend she was someone else.

She asked me what I wanted, and I told her she already knew.

She looked around playfully then stepped forward. I felt her hand on the outside of my jeans, compelling me to pitch a tent in my boxers.

"Poor baby," she said. She was looking at my face.

"You should see the other guy."

"Oh, I bet." She ran her hands over my shoulders, felt my hard, tight chest.

"Oh, I betchya fucked him up good, big boy."

I assured her I had. I smiled when I thought of No Nuts' face filled with shotgun lead. Smiled so hard it hurt.

She looked around again then pulled me to the darkest corner they had.

Finally, I could feel those Percocets kicking in.

"Whaddya want, Stud?"

I told her I wanted her forbidden fruit, and we better do it quick before I changed my mind.

She nodded, told me I could have it by the way she moved

her body up and down my leg with an ancient rhythm, the only honest dancing she'd done all night.

She spoke to me slow and held her mouth open like she was offering me something I'd be a fool to pass up. "You want me baby?"

"Sure," I said. "Why not?"

She brushed her lips against mine, and I did my best to ignore what could've been light mustache stubble. Then she reached down and slid her hand into my pants, wrapped her fingers around my package.

"Oh," she said. "That's nice."

I did my best to picture the girl from Cowboy Roy's with the American flag bandana and that ass that could fit on a breakfast plate.

She pulled me toward her and told me nobody could see us.

I concentrated on those pasties while she worked my lower unit. Best-case scenario, I ended up with a free handy and a mess to clean up. Worst-case scenario, I ended up banging her then shooting myself in the parking lot.

We faced each other, and our mouths came together but did not touch. I pushed my swollen nose into her cheek, felt her warm breath against my neck.

"*Valentine!*" I heard my name in the distance.

I told her not to stop. Just a few more pulls and I'd be golden.

"Valentine, get over here, you fuck."

She shrugged, then slowed down to a complete stop.

"NO," I snapped. "*Work that wrist goddamnit!*"

"Hey, screw you." She yanked her hand from my trousers.

"Oh, c'mon," I said. But then we got a good look at each other in that unforgiving light, and my boner died faster than a two-dollar watch battery.

"Asshole." She stormed off.

Across the room, Big Tony shook his head and waved me over.

"Jesus, Valentine," he said once I got close. "Them boys fucked you up."

I was surprised as hell to see him. I asked him how he knew.

"Let's go outside."

I followed him out to Doyle's van.

Big Tony climbed in the passenger side and I climbed in the back.

Doyle turned and looked at me, said I was in bad shape.

"I thought you guys left town."

"We couldn't leave ya here like this, kid."

Big Tony turned around and said we were in this together. Said we were going to see it through.

"I'm fifty-four years old," Doyle said. "I ain't gonna spend the rest of whatever time I got left lookin' over my shoulder."

"Me either," said Big Tony.

I asked Big Tony how he knew about the gunfight.

He said, "We's just turnin' onto Blackmore when you stumbled out into the street with that hand cannon. We seen the Englishman, and we done our best to chase him down. We lost him for a while, then we picked 'em up on the highway. Doyle here run him off the road."

Doyle was shaking his head in agreement. I noticed he wore a new watch.

He asked me what kind of burner I carried, and I told him a .45.

"Holy shit, that's a big gun." Told me all he carried was a .38 Special. "Why you use a .45?"

I told him they didn't make a .46.

Doyle told me what he'd heard. Joe Parker was on a rampage on account of this money, and everyone who had anything to do with the case was dead.

I told him I already knew. I said I'd seen the security guard, told him how those sick assholes burned out his earholes with red-hot pokers.

"Jesus," Big Tony said. "That's some old-school Mafia shit right there. The Englishman done this?"

"Indeed." I told him how they stuffed Frank into a blender, the one he always hated.

"Those limberdick cocksuckers," Doyle whispered.

Big Tony said we only had one chance, we had to do it now and we had to do it right. He said once you cross that line there was no turning back.

I said the only lines I cared about were the chalklines around their dead bodies. "Well, in that case they're holed up just down the road," Big Tony said.

"*What?*" I put my hand on the door handle. "*Let's go.*"

"Hang on a minute," Big Tony said. "There at Angie's. One uh those bitches from the club. That English prick used to drill her."

"Good," I said. "Let's go." Then I took one last look around the Queen of Hearts.

We left in Doyle's van. The Vic sat in the parking lot; I left the money in the trunk along with the cooler and at least nine empty bottles of top-shelf liquor.

I held the shotgun in my lap, filled with turkey loads. Powerful enough at close range to blow a hole through a man the size of a kitchen table. And beside me was the chainsaw.

"What the hell you do with that thing anyway?" Doyle asked.

I told him Nick Valentine didn't leave home without it,

and Big Tony thought that was funny. Doyle laughed too. "*Have chainsaw, will travel.*"

"Yeah," I said, "Something like that."

Doyle romped on the pedal and the ass end jumped to the right.

"Easy big fella," Tony said.

Doyle rubbed his palms on his pants, said he just wanted to get this over with. This time tomorrow he'd be in Florida.

I sipped on the rest of the Hot Damn I'd pulled from the floorboard of the Vic. I wished I'd had something more potent, but at least it was alcohol, something I desperately needed to maintain my edge. I thought about poor Frank, and my face turned hot. That poor little bastard was never gonna sprint those stairs again with the same pride or fervor. I racked the 12-gauge and Big Tony jumped.

"Calm down," I told him.

"Shit, Valentine. You scared the fuck outta me."

I told Big Tony I was ready. I needed to see them dead for what they'd done to Frank.

"Valentine, I gotta ask. That's really a hell of a name for a dog, ain't it?"

It caught me off guard. Got me thinking about things I didn't need to think about just before I killed a man.

"Guess I done it on account of my old man. He loved the guy. Sinatra was like a god to my old man."

Big Tony nodded. Said he understood. "We's just talkin' 'bout our pops the other day, weren't we Doyle?"

Doyle nodded. "We were. Both of 'em were real pricks by the sound of it."

Big Tony agreed. He asked, "What about your old man? He gone?"

I said he was.

"What happened to him?"

175

I hadn't thought about the old man in a long time. In the hum of road, I thought about the man he was to me. Remembered only in short clips of distant memories. He was loyal, the most honest man I knew, a cop who played by the rules. Then I thought about the way he died.

"He loved being a cop," I told them. "He and Chief Caraway, they were partners. One night they interrupted a robbery." I swallowed hard and stared out the window. I felt the 12-gauge in my lap, squeezed it tight. I hadn't shed a tear for the old man in twenty years. I wasn't gonna start now.

Doyle switched lanes and got off the interstate. Turned onto Charbonneau.

I cleared my throat. "So, they interrupt this robbery and my Pops took two in the gut by some tweaked-out biker. But that didn't kill 'em. He crawled on his belly for a hundred feet and shot the cocksucker who'd just gut shot him and left him for dead. Saved Caraway's life, too."

Doyle pulled over and killed the lights. They listened to me ramble on.

"So this biker whore comes up behind him, this other guy's old lady I guess. She's all whacked out on something, who knows what? She caved in my old man's head with a splitting mall. Caraway shot her, but it couldn't bring him back.

"I was in high school. Decided I was never gonna end up like my old man. I was gonna do things my way."

"Well you been true to your word, I'll give you that," Doyle said.

We felt gusts of wind push hard against the van and listened to the sounds a car makes once you kill the engine. Dinging, hissing, an unexpected pop.

I passed the bottle up front, asked them if they wanted

a hit before we shotgunned those motherfuckers. Then we heard gunshots, fast and wild.

"What the fuck is that?"

"Holy Christ," Doyle said. "What do we do?"

I jumped from the van as Parker's crew ran out into the yard, but the Englishman stopped hard. He said something to his partner then returned to the house. Doyle was beside me; Big Tony was still in the van.

"I told him to stay put, he'd just be in the way, the fat fuck." I agreed one hundred percent. I told Doyle he should go back too.

"No, I got this," he said. I told him he should go back to the van and wait.

"Bullshit, I'll take the Englishman, you get *him*." He pointed to the one Sid called No Nuts then took off. He said killing Sid was something he had to do.

I dropped low and tried to stay in the shadows, but the full moon spotlit my every move, and the snow made it hard to walk. I scanned the street for signs of life, but it was late. Everyone slept, their furnaces working overtime. Soon their comfortable homes would be disturbed by the sounds of gunfire. There was only one house close by, where the Lexus was parked, the one I'd shot the fuck out of earlier.

As I closed in on the driveway, I watched to my left for Sid to walk out. I still had my .45 and could draw it quick. I didn't see Doyle.

When I got to the car I saw No Nuts sprawled in the front seat, covered in bandages.

Gunshots came from my left.

No Nuts twitched forward, forcing me to action as sirens wailed in the background.

I ran to the side window and adopted a shooter's stance. No Nuts couldn't turn. The tape restricted his movements, but he knew I was there; I made sure of it. I pushed the shotgun to his head and paused long enough for him to understand what was coming. "This is for Frank."

It happened fast, in a whirlwind of blood and bullets and hate. Big Tony saw the inside of the Lexus light up in a spectacular burst of orange daylight which punched holes through the inside of the windshield and blew most of No Nuts upper half out through the driver's window onto the snow.

Big Tony hit the headlights and drove to the front of the house. "Get in," he yelled. The sky behind him alive with red and blue flashes of light.

I ran to the van and dove into the passenger side.

"What about Doyle?"

Big Tony looked at me and said Doyle was a big boy, he'd find a way out.

I told him I heard gunshots.

"Yeah, I heard 'em too."

He turned the van around and left the street the way we'd come as the first cop raced passed us.

Big Tony turned the scanner up as loud as it would go, told me soon as I'd gotten out of the van they'd broadcasted the call.

"Damn that was quick. Too quick." It sounded to me like they were already on their way. We could see another set of lights coming toward us, and I watched Big Tony tap his finger on the wheel. He looked over, asked me what I thought we should do.

"I think you need to get the fuck outta St. Louis. Go to Florida or somethin'."

"Vegas," he corrected me. "I'm goin' to Vegas."

I nodded. "That's right. Go to Vegas then. Spread the money around. Live a long life. Try not to blow it all on coke."

The second cop screamed past us, sirens screeching and lights blinding us as we drove headfirst into freezing rain.

"What about you, Valentine?"

I shrugged, told him I couldn't leave anytime soon. I'd wait and see how things turned out. The more shit that went wrong, the less I cared about the money.

He said he understood, and I should feel free to give him my share if I decided not to keep it. Big Tony said he was leaving tonight, said Doyle was too.

I asked him if they'd keep in touch.

"Yeah, sure," he said. "He's got an aunt down in West Palm Beach, so I'll know where to find him."

"Well, you know where to find me too."

He nodded, said, "What're you gonna tell the Chief?"

I told him I didn't know. Maybe I'd just tell him the truth. I used my connections and I got too close. They tried to shut me down then I guess somebody shut them down.

Big Tony told me he wanted me to drop him off at his Lincoln.

"That's fine. What about Doyle's van?"

"Just leave it at the Queen." He shrugged. "Doyle'll figure it out."

We came to a parking lot where the Town Car was sitting in a corner, covered in a thick swathe of ice. I told Big Tony take care. I'd see him when I'd see him.

"You too, Valentine. Take care of yourself. Try not to drink so much, ya prick."

I responded in the same manner I always did when my drinking came into question. I smiled, and my thoughts turned to fresh liquor.

I drove the van straight to my place, figured the Vic was fine where it was. I could get it in the morning. Wouldn't be long before the sun'd be coming up.

Amish Ron was parked in front of my office, so I parked around back in the alley. I had a long morning ahead of me and didn't know how things would go with Ron.

I locked up the van and walked a block or two up the street. It was bitter; I could feel ice pellets coming down. I turned the corner and walked back down to my place. When I got close enough I tapped on the hood of the Impala. Ron jumped hard, and the door opened quickly.

"There you are, goddammit. Where the hell you been? There's cops lookin' for you, have been all night. I'm just here to give you the common courtesy to turn yourself in."

I told Ron to calm down. Said he'd better check himself before he wrecked himself.

"Jesus, Valentine, are you drunk?"

"Not near enough," I informed him.

Ron looked around like he couldn't believe we were having this conversation.

"Do you know how much trouble you're in, Nick?"

I asked him what the hell he was talking about. Told him I hadn't done anything wrong. I'd just had my home invaded, gotten my ass beat, watched my dog become an amputee, and shot a man in the face. I decided I'd have a drink.

Amish Ron stared me down and worked me over with his mind. He'd been watching my features, studying my expressions and cross-referencing them with the mannerisms he'd observed over the last couple of days.

"So, you don't know anything about the dead bodies in a house at the corner of Davidson and Whitmer?"

I squinted, thought hard. I said I didn't know what he was talking about, but I could see I hadn't sold him yet.

"Listen, you can ask around. I had a few drinks. Then my guy showed up with something that should interest you greatly."

"*A few drinks?*" It was always the little things with Ron.

"Yes, a few. Like ten. Ten is a few to me."

The Amishman was dumbfounded. He scowled and said he didn't believe me.

"You gonna stop breakin' my balls or what?"

"That depends on what you've got for me."

"How about a duffel bag full of money which I probably should have kept?"

Ron was in the process of lighting up a smoke when he stopped. He looked at me disbelieving, rolled the cigarette between his fingers.

"You're shitting me, Valentine?"

I assured him I was not. All I wanted was to get out of this cold. A drink would be nice.

"Where's the money?"

"In the trunk of my Crown Victoria." I told him where it was parked. Said I'd been drinking hard, trying to get over just shooting a man in my office. I passed out in the car. When I woke up, I decided the walk might do me good. Figured it was best I didn't drive.

"So you just left the money in the car?"

"I wasn't gonna carry it."

Ron told me that was great, he never doubted me for a second.

I told him to drive me back there and we could get it now. I said I didn't want to be responsible for it any longer than I had to.

We pulled out and Amish Ron put fire to one of those stinking Winstons, and it took everything I had not to karate chop him in the throat.

"Put down that window you crazy bastard. I'm getting cancer over here."

He laughed and shook his head, but I heard the window slide down.

The light drizzle became stronger and drove ice into the windshield.

"Getting bad out," Ron commented.

I told him that was a pretty astute observation on his part; I asked him if he wanted me to drive.

He said that was a bad idea, he had it under control.

We turned into the Queen of Hearts, desolate in the cruel morning light, and the Vic was sitting in the back by itself.

Ron got out first, and I followed him to the trunk. I put my key in the lock, popped it open, and pointed to the bag.

He shook his head, said he didn't believe it.

We transferred the bag from my trunk to his, and he told me maybe it was for the best if I didn't drive. He asked me to come with him to the house on Whitmer Road. Maybe there was someone there I could identify.

"It sounds like it could be the two that muscled you."

I knew I couldn't argue so I told him to get a move on. The way he drove it'd be noon by the time we finally arrived.

The Impala held the road as the ice fell hard and persistently, crashing into the hood and roof with razor-sharp monotony. I thought about the cash in the trunk; I was glad it was out of my hands. Money was useless if it suffocated you with the crushing weight of its history. This was money good men died for. Except that wasn't exactly true. Everybody dead had it coming with the exception of Norman

Russo. A banker who loved his house, but confided to the wrong set of ears.

Then there was Frank Sinatra, the real victim in all of this. The greatest crime he ever committed was shitting on the passenger seat of the Vic, and I'd forgiven him for that weeks ago.

"What'd you do with the shotgun, Nick?"

That damn Amishman was always trying to jam me up.

"Huh?" I did my best to avoid his questions and led him to believe I was drunker than I was.

"You said you shot What's His Nuts with a shotgun. I didn't see it in your office and I didn't see it in your car."

I told him it was No Nuts, and those fuckers must've taken the shotgun. Said I hadn't really thought about it until now.

"You look like you took a pretty good beating. Hope you's able to give some back."

"I did my best. He's got a broken hand and a busted nose. That much I remember."

"What about the other guy?"

"The one I shot?"

"Yeah, him."

"I'm pretty sure he's fucked."

"That's what shotguns do." Amish Ron took a hand off the wheel and shook another cigarette loose from the pack. If he failed to achieve a spot on the bomb squad, I was convinced he had a promising future in competitive chain-smoking. With his background and strong work ethic, Amish Ron would be a genuine contender at the World Championship of Smoking.

"One of the bodies is outside," Ron said. "This crime scene'll be fucked up."

"You know what happened?"

"We found a black Lexus in the neighbor's driveway."

He looked over at me, asked me what kind of car I'd shot at.

"Something big and powerful. It was black, but it was all beat to shit."

Amish Ron smiled. "That's it. It was in a hit-and-run earlier today. Now there's a dead body in the passenger side."

I told Ron I hoped it was the crew from my office, but I guessed we'd know soon enough.

Ron said making an ID might be kind of hard. Most of his head and neck were plastered to the inside of the car; the rest was blown out into the yard. Amish Ron said killing a man like that sounded personal.

I told Ron killing a man was always personal.

Ron nodded and changed the subject.

"What about the money?"

I'd been waiting for him to bring that up. I guess it was the cop in him, always trying to pitch me a curve ball.

I shook my head. "My source is confidential."

Ron turned onto the road, and I could see flashing lights. Camera crews were already setting up.

"Chief's going to wanna talk to you."

I said I had to talk to him too. All of these ghosts and demons from the past were coming out and needed to be put down hard.

The end of the road was roped off, and a cop on each side lifted the yellow police tape to let the car pass. There were lights connected to generators and a vast blue tent erected over the Lexus, covering the neighbor's driveway and most of the stripper's front yard. More yellow police tape surrounded the property. Ron shut the car off, asked me if I was ready.

"Let's get this over with," I said. I told him I was starving, and he promised me breakfast at Rosebud's when we were done, an idea that appealed to me.

We ducked under police tape, and I nodded to Cameron Worthy. He was wrapped in a stocking cap and scarf, adjusting his camera. I nodded, and he looked at me with surprise.

"We gotta quit meeting like this."

"No shit, Valentine. You back on the force or what?"

I shrugged and shoved my hands deep into my pockets, wished I had gloves. I told him I was just helping out. Said I didn't think the force was ready to have me back just yet.

Cameron nodded. He asked me if I'd been inside.

"Huh uh, just got here. You?"

"Yeah, pretty grisly. Probably not as bad as this guy though." He nodded at the Lexus. Cameron told me they found a sock in the floorboard filled with human teeth.

I acted surprised, but I wasn't. No telling whose teeth those were.

"What kind of asshole drives around with a sock full of teeth?" Cameron didn't have an answer. But I did.

"Hey, Nick!" I turned and Amish Ron waved me over.

"What do you make of this?"

The inside of the car was splattered with blood, bone, and hair.

"It looks like death by shotgun."

"Probably buckshot," somebody chipped in.

I defied the urge to correct him, tell them it was actually the result a 3-inch turkey load.

"Sumbitch is covered in duct tape." Ron seemed legitimately amused.

I put my head in the window and told him it looked like the same sumbitch I'd shot earlier today in my kitchen area.

Detective Beachy asked one of the techs crawling around on the ice if he was having any luck.

"You know how hard it is to find brain matter in snow? So far all I've got's what appears to be a partial jawbone."

"Nothing's impossible, son," Ron said. "Just keep lookin', you're doing fine."

Amish Ron gave a few more pep talks then walked over to Chief Caraway while I viewed the remains of No Nuts. As I watched emergency workers pull his headless torso from the car, I realized I felt absolutely nothing for the prick. I thought about that sock filled with teeth and knew killing him was the best thing I'd done since the day I saved Frank.

I discovered him on the street, gaunt and starving. He'd made an audacious escape from the hands of his abusive owner, and I took him in, did what I could to help. I'd promised him a better life, but now he was scratching at death's door in a hospital bed, and the only thing Frank had to look forward to was a powerful limp and the strong prospect of alcoholism.

The Chief called me over and put his arm around my shoulder.

"Damn you, Nicky. We were worried, son." The skin around his eyes was pink, but tough. Like raw leather pulled tight across his cheekbones. I saw tears fight to escape his warm eyes and I looked down, watched as the snow absorbed the blood.

"Ron tell you I got back some of the money?"

The Chief nodded, said he knew he could count on me. He asked me if I was coming over for Christmas with him and Barbara this year. I told him I wouldn't miss it.

Ron said the Lexus was registered to Sydney Godwin, originally from Manchester.

"That sound like the guy?"

"Yep," I said. "That's what that fuckhead called him."

I pointed to the fat headless torso wrapped in duct tape on the stretcher.

"C'mon," Amish Ron said. "After we ID this limey asshole, let's go get some breakfast."

When Ron made a break for the house, I followed him around to the back, where a uniformed officer handed us rubber gloves.

There was a stack of shoes just inside the back door area so no one tracked in any melt and compromised the crime scene.

"This where they gained access?" Ron asked the officer.

The cop yelled over the wind. "Looks that way. There's a single key in the door, no other signs of forced entry."

"How many DB we got?" A piece of siding above our heads caught the wind and dangled, then crashed back into the house.

"One female and two males. All Caucasians. All the result of gun shot wounds by the looks of it."

Amish Ron thanked him, told him he'd done a good job.

I watched Ron operate as he explored the scene methodically. He worked a grid pattern, did a visual sweep of the room. He started from the outside, worked his way in.

Detective Dan O'Shea stepped in from the garage and showed Ron a few notes he'd made.

"We got any identification on these people?"

O'Shea said, "Well, not officially. But it looks like she's the resident." He pointed with an ink pen to a dishwater blonde on the floor with a hole in her breast. "And it looks like this guy over here could be *that* neighbor." O'Shea pointed first to the man on the floor with his brains blown out, then toward the house where the Lexus was parked.

187

O'Shea got close to the stripper and took a picture with a digital camera.

"Looks like she took the hit right about *there*." I pointed toward the inside of the doorframe. I turned around and backed up close to where I assumed she'd been standing.

"She takes the hit, *here*." I pointed to my chest. "Falls back against the wall, leaves a blood trail to the floor."

O'Shea agreed with my assessment. He looked down at her arm twisted behind her back. The blood pooled toward the inside of her elbow. One eye was closed, the other open but slightly askew, just enough to see dead white. Her mouth unhinged.

"Strange way to fall," O'Shea said.

I told him it was; I said sometimes people died funny.

He laughed uncomfortably, it becoming more and more apparent my crime scene humor would never fully be appreciated.

When Ron stepped into the garage, I followed. He asked me, "This your Englishman?"

Doyle was lying on the concrete with a big hole in his face. The contents of his skull spilled across the floor like bulky curds of strawberry cottage cheese. What I could only speculate to be medium-sized chunks of brain adorned the side of an old yellow refrigerator, rust working its way up from the bottom. There was a .38 Special in his hand; he'd been taken by surprise.

"Looks like somebody blasted him twice in the head," Ron said. "Right through the cheek bone too. Boy, these assholes sure don't fuck around whenever they kill a guy."

I told Amish Ron that wasn't the guy we were looking for. "*What?*"

"It ain't him," I said. "That's not the Englishman."

"Well, son-of-bitch. You sure?"

I told him I was positive. Doyle was gone; I sat down on the hood of a Ford Taurus parked in the garage.

The detectives conversed among themselves until the Chief walked in. He told Ron the sun was coming up, and he wanted him to do a live interview on News Channel 5 in ten minutes. Ron went out to the car to get his tie.

Caraway took a seat beside me on the hood of the stripper's car and asked me about my dog.

"I won't know for uh couple of hours yet."

The Chief told me he was sorry to hear about that. Said the world would be better off without all those sick bastards in the first place. He looked me in the eye and told me I was doing God's work.

I thanked him for his kind words, explained I was here to help. As long as he could tolerate my unconventional methods I'd work for him anytime he needed me.

He thanked me for finding the money, said he knew I'd worked hard. He told me my old man would be proud of me today. I wasn't so sure.

We talked for a few minutes then left the garage. I stepped over Doyle's body and admired that watch. Considering the price he paid, I felt I owed it to him to slip it off his wrist at his funeral. It was the least that I could do.

After Amish Ron's big press conference, we drove in the ice storm to Rosebud's for world-class pancakes prepared by a man who was only one phone call away from being a registered sex offender. Be that as it may, I had to admit they were superior. I ate three right off the bat and said to keep 'em coming. I reminded him in no uncertain terms his freedom was only as secure as my next pancake.

Ron asked me what I was going to do.

"I thought about moving to some place with a beach. Right now any place sounds better than St. Louis."

He laughed, asked wouldn't I miss Rosebud's pancakes?

"Fuck Rosebud." I said I wouldn't miss getting ambushed or assaulted either. I sure as shit wouldn't miss this snow.

"I don't blame you, Nick. If I were you, I don't think I'd leave the house without a gun."

I told Ron he didn't have to worry about that.

We stopped at a gas station on the way back to the Vic, and I grabbed a container of vodka, a gallon of orange juice, and a bottle of Mad Dog 20/20.

Amish Ron dropped me off at the Vic and thanked me again for my assistance. He said I was a good cop, said the Chief thought of me like a son.

"Thanks," I said. "Great working with you too, Ron."

I climbed behind the wheel of the Vic, spun the key, cranked up the heat, and searched for the closest Styrofoam cup. I listened to the Police Interceptor warm up while I made a screwdriver. I nudged the pedal and made the pipes rumble, felt the body of the car shake with the aftershock of unrefined horsepower. I enjoyed a substantial draw from the cup as I barreled from the parking lot sideways, sliding in the ice, spinning the tires, the glass packs sounding like they were being throat fucked by a Quarter Horse as vodka and orange juice sloshed from my cup.

I drove with the sun to my left, my eyes wasted and dead. I felt the bite from the vodka, and I shook up the glass for a bit before I tried again. The last few days ran together in a distorted white haze. I went from being poor, to being rich, to being poor again.

When I got to the Animal Hospital, I hoisted the cup high and guzzled what was left. I slipped and skidded across the frozen lot.

I walked through the door and rediscovered the stunning girl I'd met yesterday. She was waiting with a smile that could heal my deepest wounds. She had blonde curls tied up in a failing bun, and she greeted me with something I'd like to think was more than just casual affection. Her smile radiated innocence and taunting sexuality.

She told me I had the toughest dog she'd ever seen.

I told her Frank had the heart of a champion then I asked about his condition.

She grinned at me proudly, dropped her chin down. Said she thought it was sweet the way a man as tough as me cared for such a tiny mutt.

"Sometimes dogs are better than people."

"Oh my God! I know. You're *so* right."

She couldn't have been older than twenty-one, and I liked the way that uniform wrapped tight around her. She saw my famished eyes and blushed. Told me I should stop that.

"What if I can't?"

She giggled uncomfortably, but not in such a bad way. My smoldering gaze forced her to shuffle papers on a desk that didn't need shuffling. The silence created a slow tension I let build.

I reached down just far enough to brush against her hand, and then I broke the awkward silence with a question about my partner.

"What about Frank?" I asked. "Is he ever gonna dance again?"

She told me that was sweet. Her voice expressed both relief and disappointment. "Come with me." When she took me by the hand, her fingers felt delicate inside my formidable grip. If I weren't so concerned for Frank's well-being, I would have swept her off her feet and thrown her passionately to the desk.

She led me down a short hall that smelled like animals and soap. We came to a room on the right with an incubator in the corner. Frank was inside, wrapped up tight in a blanket. Absorbing the potent waves of heat.

His eyes blinked hard when he saw me. He tried to bark, but his hoarse tone betrayed him. He tried again, and it was a little raspy, but it was the bark he used when he'd hear me stomp up the stairs. I'd always drive my soles into the wood with a little extra force when I got to the top. I did it just for him.

Frank sneezed, licked his lips, barked, and sneezed again. He tried to wiggle out of that blanket.

I reached to stroke his fur, and he licked my bloodstained hand. I told him I was glad to see him too.

"The veterinarian would really like you to wait a little while before you take him home. I don't think he was expecting you quite this early."

"Oh?"

She grinned, and the corners of her smile raised her cheeks up to meet her eyes.

"He wants to talk to you about his foot."

"What about it?" I asked. "Should I change his name to Tripod?"

"No, silly." She giggled, touched my arm, and a sweet scent drifted toward me. "We were able to save his foot. The doctor reattached it."

I told her that was great. "Let me know if there's anything

I can do to repay you personally. *Anything at all.*" I showed her just enough teeth to make her match my smile; I pulled Frank from the incubator and stuffed him in my coat.

"Bye, Frank!" She waved at him with her tiny fingers, and that scorching pink nail polish caught my attention.

"I think he's gonna miss you," I told her. Frank licked his lips, snorted.

She looked up at me with blond curls straining to burst free from their confines. I suppressed my urges. Thoughts of her on top of me and the expression on her face. . .

Her unmanageable curls pasted to her naked chest with sweat.

Her delicate throat moaning for me.

Her fists pounding my chest.

The way she'd squeeze me down below, drawing me deeper into her small body.

"What about you?" she asked.

She glanced down at my hand, didn't see a ring. If she noticed any blood splatter on my sleeve, she failed to mention it. "Are you gonna miss me too?"

"I might have to chop off another one of Frank's legs just to come back."

She threw her head back and laughed. She told me I was funny then she got close enough for Frank to lick her cheek.

I wanted to feel her tongue in my mouth. I needed to know if her lips tasted like flowers smelled.

I moved and let her fall into me, and for a moment our bodies pressed against each other.

We turned to leave, and she told me I should come back sometime.

I stopped at the door, Frank under one arm, and smiled. "You never know," I said. "One of these days I just might surprise you."

Then I walked toward the light that waited for me past the hospital doors and stepped into the brilliant morning sun.

I'd left the Vic running so the heat was good and strong when we sat down. I patted Frank's little head and set him on the floorboard so he could lick clean what was left of Cowboy Roy's chili.

While chili may not be the best post-operative snack, Frank was durable. We shared a bond that transcended the standard relationship of man and dog.

I thought of Frank as my wingman.

I asked him how he liked that chili.

EPILOGUE

Sunlight melted the snow in soft patches at the house on Whitmer Road.

Tree trimmers and electricians worked to cut down limbs and restore power to the houses damaged by the ice storm. A one-ton truck the color of rust lifted a worker in the air with a bucket to remove a branch from a downed power line. He cut it free with his saw, and it fell to the frozen street where his grounds man disposed of it. The wood chipper lurched brutally as the limbs fed through and belched out wads of splinters and ice. The sound of the powerful chipper mixed with the roar of chainsaws up and down the neighborhood streets blended to create a potent symphony with enough excitement to arouse even the most grizzled lumberjack.

Next to the empty house wrapped in police tape sat an overgrown lot with piled-up brush and a few trees that could just as soon be cut down as let grow. Voices shouting in the distance fought to be heard over heavy equipment.

Inside the garage a Ford Taurus rocked from side to side until the trunk finally popped open and creaked eerily in the stillness of the room. English Sid climbed out, making sounds of pain and discomfort.

He'd been curled up for twelve hours, maybe more. He'd counted on the incompetence of the police department to overlook such an obvious detail as the car, which was fine.

I'd counted on that too.

He looked out through the windows in the top of the door then stumbled toward the chalk outline of Doyle's body. He walked by the fridge, and I stepped out of the darkness and struck him in the right ear with a pulverizing blow from a roofing hammer.

Sid went down to the floor and his head found concrete. Blood raced from his ear, ran into his eye, covering the white with a thin veneer that looked like juice from crushed cherries.

"That really looked like it hurt," I told him.

I wedged the claw end of the hammer in his mouth and stood up, yanked him hard. I fishhooked the inside of his cheek, bent his teeth in, and forced him to choke on blood. His cheek ripped loose as I pulled him to the front of the Taurus and bound his hands securely.

If there was one thing I believed in firmly it was good-quality rope. When in the market for good rope, one must consider such characteristics as tensile strength and flexibility. You don't want your subject to slip out of the knot you tied because you grabbed some cheap rope off the dollar shelf. Superior quality is what I demand in a binding rope, and a thorough knowledge of knots is an absolute must.

I rolled Sid on his back and tied him to the bumper. Blood poured from the wound, covering his face and neck like winding lines of a roadmap. Sid's ear was deformed; a chunk of his cartilage protruded out in a twisted pink knot of flesh. I asked Sid if he could hear me.

"*Remember me, asshole?* I really hope you can hear me, you English prick." I pushed him hard and his head moved. His left eye blinked, then rolled up under his eyebrow.

"Well, I'm afraid I've got some pretty bad news for you, Sid. It's all pretty fucking bad actually. I'm not really sure where to start." I rapped on the side of his head, his eye sprang open, but he couldn't focus. He drifted in and out of various levels of awareness.

"Anyway, guess I'll go head'n start with the worst news first. I want you to know I'm gonna cut your legs off with a chainsaw, Sid. Actually, it's my Stihl." I patted the little engine with my gloved hand, and Sid's leg moved forward. He mumbled pathetically.

"Ah, that's a good sign. You can't talk I guess, but at least you can understand what I'm saying. That's excellent news."

Sid continued to blink his eye, but he couldn't keep the blood out.

I stood up and walked the garage. I needed to stretch my legs after all that standing around, waiting for that prick to get out of the trunk.

I pulled my left glove off, lifted up my mask. "I gotta say, your ex-girlfriend had pretty good taste in liquor." I took a gulp of something I'd concocted in Angie's kitchen involving rum, tequila, and butterscotch schnapps. "That's one hell of a thing you did, shooting her in the tit like that." Sid groaned, tried to speak. "Is that any way to treat a lady?"

He was a savage. A brute devoid of compassion or remorse. Whatever he got he had coming.

I told Sid, "Y'know, there's just something remotely fascinating about cutting off another man's legs with a chainsaw. *Especially if he's still alive.* No, you won't like it much, but considering the circumstances, I feel like it's something that must be done." Sid tried to move. "All that's required is a trusty saw, some good quality rope, and a little strong will."

I squatted down, looked him in the eyes. "I might also suggest a bottle of Percocet for the pain. Not for you of course, but for me. Operating a chainsaw is tough work, and it can play hell on the lower back."

Sid came to about as far as his destroyed eardrum would allow. I told him a wallop to the head like that could make a man strange for the rest of his days. Not that he had many of those left.

I went through a checklist in my head.

Chainsaw, *check.*

Good-quality rope, *check.*

Percocet, *check.*

I'd brought along on old cassette player that I placed on top of the fridge. My intentions were to set the mood with some background music, create a little ambiance. I stepped on Sid's ankle with all my weight and rolled it back and forth against the concrete. I asked him how he felt about Old Blue Eyes.

Snow fell in small pieces, drifting off branches far above, as tree trimmers notched trees and dropped limbs. The wood chipper barked obnoxiously but kept chipping, chewing up trees and making sawdust that blew in the wind and landed on top of yesterday's snow.

There'd be no one around to hear the chainsaw howl when I started it up and filled the garage with the intoxicating aroma of 2-stroke smoke.

For a brief period I worked as a chainsaw salesman so I knew my way around a saw pretty well.

I explained to Sid that he wasn't going to like this part very much, but I assured him he'd brought it upon himself by being such an asshole. I told him soon he'd be joining his pal No Nuts.

"Oh, that's right, you probably didn't know. I blew his head off with a shotgun earlier. I shot him twice today actually, if you count the first time."

Sid tried to grin, tried to speak. He gagged and spit blood, said Johnny was dead already.

I shrugged, said maybe he had a point. "*But still,*" I said. "We coulda worked together, split the money. But no, you sons-of-bitches had to start chopping people up and filling their socks with teeth."

Sid drew a hard breath and held his right eye open long enough for blood to run down his chin then fall onto his chest and disappear down his shirt.

"Don't even think about begging."

He nodded slowly like he understood. Drove his eyebrows together hard.

"I'm gonna walk you through this, Sid." And I began a step-by-step tutorial of how I'd go about dismembering him. I used my practiced narrative, which was more than he deserved, but it took me back to my salesman days and those were the best days of my life.

"You see, a chainsaw cuts best when it's operated at full throttle. And it's always in good form to bring the bar in straight and even. If you cut using the top of the guide bar, it's important to exercise caution because the chain tries to push the saw back towards you, and failing to utilize proper form could result in a *kickback.*"

I told Sid nobody likes a kickback.

I continued the lesson. "If you use the bottom of the guide bar to cut, the saw pulls itself toward the muscle and bone, and the front edge of the saw provides a natural rest while cutting. This action gives the operator better control of the saw and is generally the preferred method among lumberjacks and arborists alike."

Sid began to mumble. He was finally beginning to realize the full potential of this sales pitch. I told Sid it was time to get to it, and I hoped there was a special place in Hell for assholes like him that used other people's heads as ashtrays.

Using my right thumb, I slid the on/off switch down into the choke position and engaged both the Throttle Trigger and the Throttle Interlock Release. I gave the saw a good shake, yanked the cord. I gave the Stihl another pull, and this time the carburetor quickly filled with gas as the choke did its job. It almost turned over.

Sid tried to kick, but I'd anticipated such uncooperative behavior and secured his feet to the end of an old wooden bench with rope.

I hit play on the radio and waited for the big band to fire up those magnificent brass instruments and come to life. The chainsaw clutched in my firm uncompromising grip, the pull cord dangling, teeth waiting to chew flesh and marrow. Frank Sinatra started belting out *New York, New York* in that forceful, authoritative voice that commanded respect.

I sang along with the Chairman of the Board as the Stihl roared to life on the third pull.

"*Start spreading the news. . .*" I dropped the splatter shield on my facemask and pushed the MS 270 Wood Boss into the tender meat of Sid Godwin's left quadriceps. The Boss sank further into the muscle, and a gleaming flash of red colored my shield in quick random bursts as I sawed through an artery and the bottom of the chain bit into the outside of his femur.

Sid's body jumped and bucked, creating a challenge to say the least, so I offered him an earnest look that conveyed my cordial sympathies, and then I pushed the *attack* part of the bar deep into the exposed meat.

As I felt the teeth chew bone, the severed arteries pumped

generous quantities of blood into the air, and I had to let off the trigger to clear my mask. Squatting down gave me the opportunity to closely inspect my work, as rapid forceful spurts continued to pump copious amounts of his life-force, painting the garage door opener above us.

Sid's eyes showed white, his body jerked viciously. The front of the Taurus shifted as blood ran from his foaming mouth, the end of his tongue bitten off. He choked and bled and died hard on the concrete.

O utside the garage, a white Chevy van with a crushed grill was parked in front of the house. Signs on the van advertised Hesemann Landscape & Supply on each side. There were two orange cones behind the van and one in front.

Nobody thought twice about orange cones.

I carried my trusty Stihl in the plastic case in one hand, the other hand the radio.

Frank was waiting in the driver's seat, and he danced around excitedly, still favoring the foot, but his spirits were higher than I'd expected.

I told him to scoot over then I climbed behind the wheel. An aftershock from the painkiller sent a ripple of warm heat crawling up my spine.

We left the dead stripper's house as the night came hard and sucked the energy from the day like a thousand-horsepower vacuum. The dark road was crawling with hungry people eager to escape their lives, toiling down the highway in their gas-powered metal coffins, and searching for deliverance in a bottle, pipe, or a bag of white dope.

The lights of St. Louis called to me in a voice like broken glass. I knew in the darkest part of the city, people were shooting heroin and shooting each other. Women were getting raped, children were being beaten and molested. Tweakers robbed credit unions for plastic gangsters, and men even cut up other men in empty garages for the things they'd done to have it end that way.

Frank rode on my lap all the way to Blackmore, and I parked the van in the alley. I removed the magnetic signs and flung them in the back.

I leaned into the van and moved things around, finally started taking an inventory of what Doyle had back there. When I looked inside a roll of carpet, the oxygen was sucked from my chest.

"Doyle, you old son-of-bitch." I found stacks of cash in a wooden box under a stack of floor tiles, at least ten thousand inside a rubber boot, more than I could count hidden inside a stack of cones.

I grabbed a huge yellow bag I could throw over my shoulder and packed it with cash. It was the bag previously used to transport Doyle's revolting suits back and forth to the cleaners.

I expected the image of Doyle's blown-apart face would haunt me longer than I wanted it too, then I thought about that cocksucker I'd just cut in half and left tied to the bumper of a Ford Taurus.

Chief Caraway wouldn't look too hard, and Amish Ron would just figure Sid got coming what was owed.

"Ready, Frank?" I walked around to the front and grabbed that little shit. When I looked under the seat my eyes came to rest on a stunning discovery, and I laughed hard enough to damage at least three of my internal organs. That fucking Doyle would steal anything.

I carried the chainsaw in my left hand. My right held a big purple dildo.

I stopped by the staircase and let Frank scout the area for the best place to piss, shit, or both. He yelped when he put pressure on his foot, and I thought of what a tough little bastard he must be to withstand such trauma and recover so quickly.

Frank lifted his leg and fired short bursts of golden piss into the snow.

We stood at the bottom of the stairs and looked at each other. We'd both been beaten and abused. We'd seen the worst mankind had to offer and fought back at their level.

I shifted my weight and got a better grip on the Stihl, got a better grip on the dildo, too. I asked Frank if he was ready, and he barked, sneezed, and snorted.

"Let's go, Frank." I drove my boot heels down into the wood as my Yorkshire terrier took off. His injuries hampered his performance to an extent, but you could never take away his passion for stair climbing.

ACKNOWLEDGEMENTS

This book would not have been possible without the help and support of the following. Thank you: Melissa, for the love and support and encouragement; Scott Phillips, for meeting me in the coffee shop that day and inspiring me to create worlds; Stona Fitch, my first editor, for making this book what it is; Stacia Decker, my amazing agent, for telling me to go with my gut; Jon Bassoff, at New Pulp Press, for *believing* and for giving me the freedom to tell the story I wanted to tell; Laura Ramie, the artist who designed the front cover of this book, and Erik Lundy, who designed the back. It took a team of dedicated people to bring *Frank Sinatra* to life. Thanks to all of you.

Thanks also to Jedidiah Ayres, Rod Wiethop, Charlie Stella, Frank Bill, Elizabeth A. White, Sabrina Ogden, Fiona Johnson, Linda Trest, Lauren O'Brien, J. S. Woemmel, Mike Keller, Brad Wyman, and, of course, Ken Bruen.

I owe a *Special Thanks* to two of my teachers from Owensville High School. Mrs. West, for moving me into advanced English in 7th grade—for believing that a kid making straight D's might have something to offer—I have never forgotten that; and to Mrs. Steineker, my English teacher in 10th grade, who read my 16 page story out loud to the class, gave me an A, and never said anything about the cuss words.

Being a teacher is hard work and nobody ever remembers to say thank you. So, thank you.